NERD GiRLS

a CaTaSTROPHe OF NeRDiSH PROPORTiONS

Also by Alan Lawrence Sitomer

The Hoopster

The Hoopster: A Teacher's Guide

Hip-Hop High School

Hip-Hop Poetry and the Classics

Homeboyz

The Secret Story of Sonia Rodriguez

Nerd Girls: The Rise of the Dorkasaurus

NeRD GiRLS

a CaTaSTROPHE OF NeRDiSH PROPORTiONS

ALan LawRence SiTomeR

DISNEP • HYPERION BOOKS
NEW YORK

Dedicated to the Nerd Girls who fill my world with love:
SBS, QBS, TRS & YY (plus the Ga-Ga'z)

acknowledgments

Is it even possible to express the deep levels of dorkasaurus
gratitude I have for the inimitable Wendy Lefkon and the
incomparable Al Zuckerman? I love you guys! You're the best.

Copyright © 2012 Alan Lawrence Sitomer

For information address Disney·Hyperion Books,
114 Fifth Avenue, New York, New York 10011.

Printed in the United States of America
Reinforced binding

First Edition
10 9 8 7 6 5 4 3 2 1

G475-5664-5-12135

Library of Congress Cataloging-in-Publication Data
Sitomer, Alan Lawrence.
Nerd Girls: a catastrophe of nerdish proportions/by Alan Lawrence Sitomer.—1st ed.
p. cm.
Summary: As a punishment for the perpetual infighting, the Nerd Girls and the
ThreePees (Pretty, Popular, Perfect) must compete together in the Academic Septhalon.
ISBN 978-1-4231-3997-3
[1. Middle schools—Fiction. 2. Schools—Fiction. 3. Competition (Psychology)—
Fiction. 4. Self-esteem—Fiction. 5. Humorous stories.] I. Title. II. Title:
Nerd Girls two. III. Title: Catastrophe of nerdish proportions.
PZ7.S6228Nf 2012
[Fic]—dc23
2011035216

Visit www.disneyhyperionbooks.com

SUSTAINABLE FORESTRY INITIATIVE
Certified Fiber Sourcing
www.sfiprogram.org

THIS LABEL APPLIES TO TEXT STOCK

hree things I love: chocolate, laughing, friends.

Three things I hate: girls who think they're better than me because they're prettier than I am, public speaking, jokes about my body.

Now all I had to do was translate that into Spanish for Mrs. Rolanda before the end of the period. No problemo, right? I mean, kicking butt on simple classroom assignments is just what nerds like me do. Put a tennis racket in my hand and I'm a pickled squid; give me a pencil and sit me at a desk and I turn into Michael Jordan.

Plus, not to toot my own horn, but note the proper usage of a semicolon in the sentence above. Uh, hello, that's like nerd to the power of nerd (*Nerd*^{Nerd}) stuff right there. Sure, I might lie about my official weight, but when it comes to booky-school stuff, things click.

Unfortunately, however, right at the moment I was preparing to nail my translation assignment *en español*, my pencil tip broke. So I did what any normal kid would do: I walked up to the front of the room to use the electric sharpener.

But I'm not just any kid; I'm a squeaker. That means when I journey across a classroom filled with students silently working at their desks, my thighs rub together and sing songs like "The Star-Spangled Banner."

I cruised up the aisle between my quiet, lost-in-study classmates, my pants yodeling the whole time. Three kids raised their eyes.

Note to self: never wear corduroys again.

"Escribe, por favor," Mrs. Rolanda crisply instructed in her perfect accent. Our dark-haired Latin American teacher always tried to speak to us in Spanish to better develop our ear for the language.

The kids who'd looked up smiled, looked back down, and returned to their assignment.

Second note to self: make time next summer to learn to walk as if you had a cantaloupe between your knees. Really, I don't know why it hadn't dawned on me to master this ability sooner.

I jammed my yellow pencil into the black hole of the electric sharpener and gazed at the multicolored Flags of the World poster hanging on the white classroom wall. While the lead of my number two buzzed its way to razorlike sharpness, my thoughts drifted to how all my life people have found me worth smiling at. Folks find me funny. Not as in *Har-har, watch me, I'm being humorous right now* funny, but rather *I just tried to do THIS, but instead I accidentally just did THAT, and har-har, the rest of the world is now laughing at me* funny. For example...

Once, while solving an equation at the front board for pre-algebra, I tripped over my feet, fell to the ground, and nearly poked out my eye with the dry-erase marker. When I popped up, I had rug burns on my ear and a huge line of squiggly blue ink running sideways across my cheek.

Everyone in the room laughed. Even the teacher.

Not very professional of her to chortle at a student's misfortune, if I do say so myself.

Another time, I used a bathroom stall that had run out of toilet paper and "adapted" by using a sheet of notebook paper to finish my business.

It jammed the toilet.

Now, whenever I see any of the custodians, they giggle at me with a *There goes the girl who wipes herself with homework* look on their faces.

Do I need to go on? I mean, I know I was born with a body shaped like a lopsided mango, but still, now that cloud computing can store my entire digital life in the invisible filing cabinet of cyberspace, you'd think someone could actually invent a stupid pair of pants that fit. A little rubbing sound is one thing; having my jeans be considered for an instrument in the eighth-grade orchestra is entirely another.

Pah-thetic.

Worst of all, though, I know Kiki Masters is going to write all about my musical *pantalones* in the Slam Book I just spied on her desk. Knowing Kiki, she's probably already filled eight pages' worth of stuff about me in that thing.

Can I just say how much I hate Slam Books? What evil person invented these beasts, anyway? Really, who takes a blank notebook, fills it with insults, and then passes it around school so that a lot more people can write nasty, hurtful things about the other kids they go to class with? And it's all done anonymously. No one ever signs their name in a Slam Book; you just flame people, then pass it along.

So lame.

However, when I saw the Slam Book on Kiki's desk a moment ago as I made my way to the pencil sharpener, I didn't get angry. Or riled up. Or excited to participate in some stupid middle-school ritual. Nope, not at all. Instead, my stomach did a backflip off the high dive, then fell like a stone to the floor. I could just imagine all the ugly things being written about me.

Maureen's a LOSER.

Maureen's blood type is lard.

You want to know Maureen's belt size? Equator.

Har-har, everyone's a comedian.

Okay, no, I am no teen magazine cover girl. But I'm not a need-two-school-desks-tied-together-to-sit-down plumparoo, either. I'm sort of in that kind of *flabby/somewhat round/really believes in the power of chocolate cupcakes to ease emotional pain* zone of body types. Yet still, the way people call me names, you'd think I was a beached walrus.

Of course, the main name-caller is Kiki. She and I have a "history" together. As the leader of the ThreePees (the Pretty, Popular, Perfect girls; thus the name ThreePees), Kiki has been torturing me for years. However, earlier this school year, I finally stood up to her and fought back. Basically, Kiki and her two pet ding-dongs, Brittany-Brattany and Sofes O'Reilly, ThreePees number two and three, had tried to make the spleen of the new girl, Allergy Alice Applebee, explode by overexposing her to stuff she was highly allergic to. Their plan was to publicly humiliate her in the center of the lunch area, where every kid in the eighth grade could see some sort of internal-organ explosion happen live.

But I saved Alice. Saved her big-time. That's what lit the fuse of friendship between me and her and Barbara "Beanpole" Tanner, a closeness that has now grown into full-on NFF status.

I guess every nerdcloud's got a silver lining, right?

None of us dorkasauruses are fashion models. And no, not a one of us is a little pink princess, either. We're just quirky, do-well-in-school, socially awkward, sit-in-the-back-of-the-cafeteria-during-lunchtime, get-laughed-at-by-other-kids eighth graders at Grover Park Middle School, in Grover Park, California.

Imaginative name for our school, huh? Kind of like naming a new dog Puppy.

I took a deep breath and tried to sigh out my anxiety, but on the inside, my tummy nervously gurgled. Lord knows what other kinds of nasty stuff Kiki's Slam Book was saying. Not just about me, but about my two bestest comrades as well.

Beanpole's bra size is pavement.

Alice's glasses are so thick she can see the future.

Barbara is so clumsy she got tangled up in a cordless phone.

That's what life is like for us. Despite all of the anti-bully stuff the school tries to preach, there's still a social ladder, and nerds are at the bottom. One notch above sludge. Of course the cool kids never even pass us those Slam Books to write in, anyway. We're the kids who get written about, not the writers.

It hurts. A lot.

With my pencil sharpened and my jaw tense, me and my melodious pants squeaked back to my desk. In Spanish class, I had the good fortune (NOT!) to be assigned to sit at the desk right behind Kiki. As I walked by, even though it was half covered by her English-Spanish dictionary, I saw it again: SLAM BOOK. Just then I saw her write something in it and trade a smirky glance across the room with her perpetual partner-in-crime Brittany-Brattany.

I'm sure they were laughing at me. They were always making rude comments and snickering at me. That's when I made the decision.

I would steal their Slam Book.

I had to. Not just for me but for all the kids who were having cruel and mean and insensitive things written about them. I thought about Brace Face Stace, a girl with so much metal in her mouth she could have wired a chicken coop. I thought about Wandering Eye-leen, a girl who always had her head turned to the left when she talked to you, and you could never tell if she was paying attention to what you were saying or gazing at a bluebird in a tree twenty yards over your shoulder. I thought about Four-and-a-half-finger Freddy, a kid who had sliced off half of his index finger playing with a circular saw in his father's garage when he was eight years old. Oh, the can't-quite-pick-every-booger-in-his-nose jokes that he's had to endure.

Yep, I would steal that Slam Book. I would steal it and then I would throw it away.

But how? I needed a plan.

"Silencio, por favor," Mrs. Rolanda snapped at a couple of

boys in the back row who had dared to whisper. Mrs. Rolanda ran a tight ship. Not only did she speak to all of her students in Spanish, but she required us to respond in Spanish as well (because how else were we going to learn the language, right?). And every night we had five new vocabulary words to learn. Plus, just recently, she had started making us carry a Spanish slang book so that we could learn some of the common phrases people who spoke the language often used.

Things like, *¿Qué pasa?* which means "What's up?" or *¡No manches!* which means "Get outta here!" Stuff like that.

Even though I was supposed to be translating my sentences, all I could think about was how to get that Slam Book from Kiki. I know some people think I'm comfortable with who I am and how I look, because I'm sort of loud and opinionated—okay, even obnoxious—but on the inside, I'm, well...this is hard to admit, but I'm insecure. Like I'm always worried that people are talking about me behind my back or are making jokes about my appearance and stuff like that. I say I don't care, but really I do. And I pretend it doesn't bother me, but really it does. My mom says I should just let it go and forget about girls like Kiki Masters, but when I saw Kiki make yet another entry in that Slam Book, I just felt like I had to do something about it.

After all, if you don't stand up for yourself in this world, who is going to stand up for you? My mom taught me that, too.

Wow, though, I thought. Kiki had some guts to be writing in a Slam Book so out in the open in the middle of class like that. I mean, between Mrs. Rolanda's general strictness and our school's zero-tolerance policy toward student-on-student harassment, if she had gotten caught with that notebook, she would have been in big trouble. Yet still she scribbled her insults, wrote down her rumors, and marked down all her hurtful, nasty lies, as if they were actually some kind of homework assignment or something.

Hmm . . . how to do this? Getting that thing from Kiki without the teacher seeing me, and without causing a ruckus, would take scheming. It would take grace. It would take a carefully calculated plan involving some sort of well-executed maneuver, like I was an elite member of SEAL Team Six going into enemy territory in the dark of night.

I leaned forward and snatched the Slam Book.

After ripping it off Kiki's desk, I hastily hid the notebook under a few sheets of paper on my own desk and quickly pretended to be hard at work before Mrs. Rolanda even raised her eyes from the papers she was grading.

Screw grace. Who had the patience?

Ha-ha, I now had the goods. And what was Kiki going to do, raise her hand and tell the teacher I had just stolen her notebook?

"Mrs. Rolanda, Mrs. Rolanda, Maureen just stole my notebook!"

OMG, was she suicidal? Once the teacher saw the kind of things Kiki was writing about me and my friends, her head was going to roll way more than mine would.

The whole class turned around.

"En español, Kiki," Mrs. Rolanda said. *"Dime en español."*

Kiki rolled her eyes. *"Maureen-o just stole-o my notebook-o."*

Mrs. Rolanda shook her head. After eleven years of teaching at this school, she was used to kids like Kiki thinking they could just add an O to the end of everything as a way of getting by. She turned her attention to me.

"*¿Cuál es el problema? ¿Esto es cierto, Maureen? ¿Tomé sin permiso el cuaderno de Kiki?*"

Though I didn't understand all the words she'd said, I did know that *cuaderno* meant notebook.

"*Sí,*" I began, ready to admit my crime. "*Pero...*" I said as I slowly began to slide Kiki's Slam Book out from underneath my papers. I mean, even though I wasn't a snitch, if Kiki wanted the teacher to see all the cruel and nasty stuff she'd been writing, what was I going to do?

I pulled the notebook out, glanced at the cover, and prepared to hand it over to our teacher so that Kiki could get what was coming to her. That's when the shock hit me.

It didn't say SLAM BOOK on the front; it said SLANG BOOK.

Gulp. I'd misread it.

Mrs. Rolanda glared. "*Señorita, estoy esperando una respuesta.*"

She was waiting for an answer. *Double gulp.* What to do?

Now, sure, I could put small, simple sentences together like "My name is Maureen" (*Me llamo Maureen*) or "I like the hamburger" (*Me gusta la hamburgesa*), but my language abilities were nowhere near good enough to explain to Mrs. Rolanda that I had gotten the wrong idea about Kiki's notebook, thought she was spreading vicious rumors about me and my friends, and planned to throw the Slam Book into the trash, so that no one else's feelings would get hurt. I mean, a person would practically have to be bilingual to explain that.

But, of course, I had to say something. After all, Mrs. Rolanda was expecting *una respuesta*, an answer. And I could tell by the way her dark brown eyes were lasering in on me that she was getting madder and madder by the minute.

"*Usted verá como un pollo,*" I replied nervously. Translation: "You look like a chicken."

Okay, okay, I admit it, I panicked. And messed up a few words, too. But like I said, I was nervous.

For the next five days I was assigned after-school detention. My task was to write the following sentence on the board two hundred times each day: **No robare las cosas que pertenecen a otros estudiantes y mi maestra no parece ave de corral.**

Translation: I will not steal the property of other students, and my teacher does not look like poultry.

Does stuff like this happen to other kids, too?

"**D**on't you just love your new cell phone, Maureen?" Beanpole asked as she pushed a bunch of buttons.

"Well, I don't want to French-kiss it like you do yours," I replied. "Ya think maybe you can put that thing away for, like, five minutes? I thought we were having a conversation here."

"Sure," she said, but I could tell she didn't really want to. Slowly, Beanpole placed her new cellie back inside her gray-and-pink backpack, but of course she did it in a way that let her still spy the screen, as if she were expecting a text message from the president or something. Truth was, there was no cell service where we were sitting.

"I mean, I guess I could let bygones be bygones," I admitted. "But I don't trust them. I just know the ThreePees are gonna try to get us."

"You're being paranoid," Beanpole assured me. "That whole

Slam Book thing, you do realize you made it all up in your head, right?"

"Whatever," I said as I returned to my lunch. *Mmm, Twinkies.*

Statistically speaking, very few nonchocolate foods rank higher on the taste-bud pleasure scale than Twinkies. And if bacon was taken off the list, ladies and gentlemen, we might have a winner.

"I thought you were, you know, trying to watch what you ate," Beanpole said in a friendly, noncritical tone.

"Yeah, well, I've been kind of yo dieting these past few weeks," I confessed.

"Don't you mean yo-yo dieting?" she said.

"Nah, it's been pretty one-sided lately."

Beanpole watched as I enjoyed another bite of my midday cuisine (gooey white cream injected into a tube of yellow-colored cake? Come on, how genius is that?). She smiled, warm and kind.

Beanpole was always warm and kind. And friendly and considerate, too. Could there be anything more annoying?

And in her kindest way, she said, "But you were doing so well on your diet there for a while."

"Diets, like rules, are meant to be broken," I insisted as I popped the last bite of Twinkie into my mouth. "Mmm," I said. "Finger-lickin' good. And trust me, nobody ever licks their fingers after eating celery stalks."

Again, Beanpole smiled, gentle and nice. Didn't she know that when the space invaders came they were going to eat the gentle and nice people first?

Essentially, I am short and squat, and Beanpole is tall and thin. I am sarcastic and skeptical; Beanpole is cheerful and optimistic. I am moody, indecisive, and greatly lacking in self-esteem; Beanpole is outgoing, generous, and ready to try anything. If it's true that opposites attract, then she and I are magnetized.

"Aw, you can't give up on yourself, Mo," Beanpole said. "Remember, you're all you've got."

"Yeah, and you just happen to"—*Wheeesh-whooosh. Wheeesh-whooosh*—"have a lot."

I glared at the girl sitting next to me, the one who had just made the comment.

"Especially," she added, grinning from ear to ear, "when it comes to the size of your butt."

Remember the Allergy Alice girl I mentioned, the one I'd saved? Well, that is the third member of our flock. Q is her name, at least that's what I call her, and she is...well, how do I say this nicely?

Q is a freak.

I'd started calling her Q a few months ago, because calling someone Allergy Alice every time you want to speak to her is just too much of a mouthful; she needed a shorter name. Besides, everything the girl says or does is a mental, medical, or social mystery, like some sort of giant question mark, so the name Q made sense.

And that *Wheeesh-whooosh. Wheeesh-whooosh* sound? It came from the NASA-approved scuba tank she always carried around with her.

All right, it isn't a real scuba tank. In reality, it's an inhaler filled with protein inhibitors that are supposed to keep her pancreas from oozing out her ear or something like that.

Essentially, Q has a few allergies, but only to small, rare, hard-to-encounter things—like water, air, and grass. Fact is, I've seen a few weirdwads in my day, but Q is the strangest, most offbeat, most peculiarest kid I've ever met.

It's what I most like about her. Q is who she is, and she is it all the time. She just doesn't care what other people think.

Q wears scarves in eighty-eight-degree weather—and doesn't care what other people think. Q attaches a tissue dispenser to her belt loop—and doesn't care what other people think. Q uses a spork to eat her lunch, finding "the functionality of a spoon-fork combo both efficient and environmentally conscious."

What guts. I mean, who at this school just can be who they are without worrying about what everyone else thinks? Sure, Q is a kook, but she is also the kid least likely to give in to peer pressure, which, when I really think about it, might make her the least kooky kid on campus.

Bizarre how that makes sense, right?

Anyway, put together, me, Q, and Beanpole made up the Nerd Girls. Feared by all we were not.

"*Aachoo!*" Q sneezed and then pulled out a tissue from her belt-loop holster. Lunch for her today consisted of boiled carrots and skinless apples with a few wheat-free, gluten-free, flavor-free crackers tossed in for good measure. Some kids are lactose intolerant; Q is any-element-on-the-periodic-table intolerant.

"Is this bothering you?" Beanpole asked, holding up a tuna sandwich that had been made in the shape of a bald eagle.

Beanpole's mom always prepared her daughter's food around themes and motifs. Today's were courage and bravery.

Don't ask.

"No, it's not the sandwich," Q answered. "It's all the dust in here."

For some reason, Beanpole had decided that the three of us should eat lunch indoors today. Way indoors. Like inside-the-art-classroom indoors. I had stopped asking questions about stuff like this a while ago, figuring that, hey, when you're friends with whack jobs, you do wacky things.

"You need to leave?" Beanpole asked.

"Nah," Q replied. "Aside from this lumpy chair, I like the atmosphere."

"You're sitting on a paintbrush," I informed her.

"Oh." Q lifted her rear, picked up the paintbrush, and looked at the bristles. "I was wondering why my tush felt all prickly."

A moment later, Q put the paintbrush right back underneath her butt.

"You're still gonna sit on it?" I asked.

"It's kind of like a bristly massage," she replied. "And tingles are good for my pulmonary circulation."

Yup, every day a new adventure.

I gazed around the art room. Paint cans, half-finished ceramic sculptures, fans to dry papier-mâché projects, all kinds of cheerful, arty-farty stuff filled the space. Just out of curiosity, I picked up some dweeb's nearly finished coffee cup and noticed that it was decorated with yellow smiley faces.

"You know," I said philosophically, "I don't see why kids our age are always supposed to be cheery and blissful and popping with joy all the time. I mean, the only thing I'm popping with is zits."

Beanpole, however, wasn't listening. Instead, her eyes were glued to her phone. She checked for a new text message.

Nothing.

"Can I just say, for the record, that I love my new phone?" she remarked. "Alice, do you love your new phone?"

"The plastic casing makes my ears itch. I have to talk on" —*Wheeesh-whooosh. Wheeesh-whooosh*—"speaker with it."

"May I continue with the point I was trying to make?" I asked as I reached for the apricot I'd packed for lunch.

Well, the apricot strudel.

"We need to be on guard against an attack from the snobwads."

"It really bothers me that my mom doesn't go out," Q interjected, nibbling on a carrot. "I mean, she has absolutely no life outside of worrying about me. It's like her entire existence revolves around me."

"Are we not going to discuss the ThreePees?" I asked.

"That's because she loves you, Alice," Beanpole said. "And she's concerned that something might happen to you."

"I'll take that as a no," I said, even though neither of them was acknowledging me.

"But I'm stronger than she thinks I am," Q said. "I mean, I'm not an invalid."

"You get light-headed from corn," I said, jumping into their conversation. Hey, if you can't beat 'em, join 'em, right? "Not exactly the stuff of Supergirl there, Q."

"Well, I need to do something. She's sacrificed enough for me these past couple of years. Too much." Q paused and considered it. "Yep, I'm gonna do something."

"What?" I asked. Almost nobody on campus knew the real truth about Q, but Beanpole and I did. There had been an accident, a terrible car crash, in which Q's father and sister had died. Q's mother wasn't in the car at the time, but Q was. Right in the backseat. Incredibly, she survived.

But she was the only one. Stuff like that'll mess you up.

"I don't know what I'm gonna do," Q told us. "But I'm gonna do something. I have to. It's my mom."

Q used to hide her emotions and bury her feelings, but ever since she came clean about the guilt of surviving, and feeling as if the car accident were her fault, she's turned into some sort of fountain of honesty. At least among us, that is. To the outside world, Q is still a semi-odd recluse, but with Beanpole and me she is a straight shooter. Like for example, if she likes your purple T-shirt, she'll tell you, "Cool purp shirt." But if she thinks your green flip-flops look weak, she'll tell you, "Lame-o foot canoes . . . Try a new set of toe kayaks."

Yeah, sometimes you have to decode what she's talking about, but still, she tells it like it is. Me, I struggle with honesty and expressing my real feelings. I mean, my mom could put on forty-five pounds and walk around the house knocking picture frames off the table with her butt, and still I'd say things like, "Put on weight? Nope, haven't noticed a thing. But perhaps you could pass the doughnuts."

Sarcasm's more my thing. I blame television.

"You know," I said, thinking about this, "I say we make a

pact to be truthful with one another. Really honest. Beanpole, tell me something honest."

Beanpole raised her eyes and thought deeply about the question. "I love my new phone."

"How profound. I see Nobel prizes in your future. Q, how 'bout you?" I said. "Tell me one honest thing, just one truthful thing about this whole mixed-up, crazy universe."

"Your gluteus says *Aardvarks* on it," she replied. "*Aardvarks* is a"—*Wheeesh-whooosh. Wheeesh-whooosh*—"funny word."

I stood, put my hands on my hips, and turned to show the lettering on my backside.

"Might I point out that these are the new, Capri-style school athletic pants I'm wearing?" I answered. "You know, trying to show some school spirit over here."

"Aardvarks."

"Don't say that."

"Aardvarks."

"Less funny the second time."

"Actually, it was the fourth," Q answered. "Accurate statistics are important to me."

Wheeesh-whooosh. Wheeesh-whooosh.

"Aardvark. Fifth time."

Deep breaths, Maureen, I told myself. *Deep breaths.*

"Well, what's wrong with being an Aardvark, anyway? I like being an Aardvark," Beanpole declared. Then, to emphasize her point, she stood like George Washington about to make a speech at Valley Forge. "After all, I am who I—" *BAM!* Beanpole smashed her head into a shelf on the wall, banging her noggin so hard I thought she'd given herself a concussion.

Oh, yeah, in case I forgot to mention, Beanpole is prone to accidents the same way I am prone to cookies.

"Don't worry, don't worry, I'm okay," she declared, sitting down and rubbing the top of her cranium. "I'm okay."

"Can you guys please just tell me one thing?" I asked. "And be honest." I hesitated, reluctant to say the words aloud, even to my closest friends. "Do these pants make my thighs look, you know, like turkey drumsticks?"

Beanpole studied my legs. "You mean like the kind injected with hormones to plump 'em up?"

I glared.

"No, not at all," Beanpole said, backpedaling. "Not at all."

"You are so unconvincing." I reached for my backpack. "All right, can we leave now, please? We're not even supposed to be in here."

"But they never lock the door," Beanpole said.

"The lock's busted," Q said, smelling her carrot stick before taking another bite. "Whole school knows it."

"That doesn't mean we're allowed in here," I said. "And why do you smell your carrot sticks before you eat them?"

"Aardvark."

"Well, if we get caught in here," I said, "you know we're going to get into trouble."

"Not if we don't mess anything up," Beanpole said.

"Aardvark. Ninth time."

"Why are you, Barbara Beanpole Tanner, the number one rule follower of the century, defending our presence here?" I asked. "Besides, the bell's going to ring, and I don't want to be late for class. Now, come on, enough with this. Let's go."

"We can't," Beanpole replied, remaining seated. "Not yet."

"Why?" I asked.

She looked down, clearly hiding something.

"Beeeanpole..."

"Because I invited the ThreePees here to eat lunch with us, so we could bury the hatchet."

"You did what?!" I shouted. Q's eyes popped wide open. This was clearly news to her, too. "Why would you do such a thing?"

"'Cause I wanted to make peace between us all," Beanpole said. "Kids at the same school should get along."

Q reached for her inhaler and took a few slurps. *Wheeesh-whooosh. Wheeesh-whooosh. Wheeesh-whooosh.* The ThreePees had already tormented her enough to last a lifetime, maybe even two, and even though Q had come out of her shell around us—people whom she trusted—all her life she had been ridiculed by divas like the ThreePees, kids who cared more about their pedicures than they did about global warming, and it had scarred her. After all, it's one thing not to care what other people think about the way you dress and act; it's totally another to be the piñata that brats like to smash with nastiness simply for their own entertainment.

"I already agreed that I'd let bygones be bygones," I said. "Isn't that enough?"

"That's not peace," Beanpole replied. "The tension is still off the charts whenever we're near them. I mean, just look at what happened with the Slam Book."

"But I don't want to eat lunch with them," I said. "I don't even want to go to the same school as them. I just want to, like, NOT deal with them. Ever."

"That's exactly what I mean," Beanpole answered. "This is why we need to meet and clear the air."

Q remained silent.

"Not a fan," I said. "Not a fan at all."

"Well, you can't always avoid things when you have issues with people in your life, Maureen," Beanpole said in a motherly tone. "No offense, but it's kind of immature."

"Immature? Me, immature? How would you like an injection of Twinkie cream up your nose?"

"Well, if that's not a mature way to handle conflict resolution, I don't know what is," Beanpole replied.

"Is that why you keep checking your phone?" I asked.

"Yeah, they're late," she said, cocking her head to one side. "And it doesn't make sense, either, 'cause we've been planning this for, like, three days."

"Planning what for three days? Lunch?"

"Kiki said they needed three days," Beanpole told me. "To get it all set up."

"Get what set up? Beanpole, this doesn't make any sense."

Then suddenly, it did. Once we heard the door close, followed by a loud *CLICK*, that is.

"Was that . . ." I said, looking toward the door. I crossed the room and tried the handle.

"Locked," I said.

I glanced around. There were no other doors.

"We're locked in."

You know, I don't really need any help when it comes to creating level-ten embarrassing situations for myself. However, the ThreePees were always eager to lend me a hand.

How nice of them.

Like that time I saved Q from the ThreePees, well, the way I did it was by hijacking these special peanut-butter-and-mango-marmalade sandwiches the vixens had made in order to trigger a monster allergic reaction in the new girl at school. Then, once I had the sandwiches, I quickly jammed them into my mouth so that the weapons of torment would be eliminated. Unfortunately, this act of heroism for Q turned into a personal disaster for me.

A disaster that ended up on YouTube, thanks to Brittany-Brattany.

Oh, the joy of seeing myself online running around the outdoor courtyard screaming, *"Mmmrrfft rrmmfft dmmfft!"* with a mouthful of sticky peanut butter preventing me from being able to utter an understandable word.

The story ended well for me, though. The video went viral. Pah-thetic.

Justice, though, was eventually served on the ThreePees after our school's big talent show, when those witches ended up sucking a karmic lemon good and hard. That's because my older brother, Marty, made their eyebrows fall out. Just before they took their official school yearbook photo, too. In the pics, their faces looked like Easter eggs designed by kindergartners on laughing gas.

A video of that was also posted on YouTube. It was hysterical. (At least, I thought so. Our school principal, not so much.)

Anyway, while we were thinking about letting bygones be bygones, the ThreePees were planning revenge, and now that they had double-crossed Beanpole and somehow "fixed" the lock on the door, we were sitting ducks.

I knew it, I thought. I just knew it.

An ominous voice cackled from above. I tilted my head backward and saw a window above the door frame. Suddenly, one, two, then three faces appeared.

"Well...looky what we have here. Nerdwads in the art room."

They must have been standing on a ladder. Though the glass muffled their voices somewhat, we could still easily hear them.

"Nice pants, Maureen. Is there going to be a rainstorm?" Brittany-Brattany asked about my new Capris. "Or does the weather just call for thunder thighs?"

The ThreePees let out a big, mean laugh.

"Yeah . . . or lightning hair."

Kiki and Brattany paused, then turned to stare at ThreePee number three, Sofes.

Some girls are not playing with a full deck. Sofes O'Reilly wasn't even dealt any cards.

"Huh?" Kiki asked.

"You know, lightning your hair?" Sofes explained. "Like when you use too much peroxide-based color wash and the oxidization of the follicles creates a shade of tint that's too light."

"Sofes, are you sure the chemicals you use in your hair products are safe for your brain?" Kiki asked.

"Well, if the shampoo I was using contained pyrethrin, there might be cause for concern, but they only put that in pet shampoo, to help control fleas and ticks."

Kiki rolled her eyes. "Can we please get back to the reason we're here?"

"Yeah . . . payback!" Brattany lifted up her camera-phone and prepared to record us on video.

"Oh, Nerd Girls, I hope you like art collages," Kiki said. "Because you are about to become one."

"On YouTube!" Brattany added with fiendish joy.

"But you said we were going to bury the hatchet," Beanpole called up to them.

"The only thing that is getting buried today, dorko, is YOU!" Kiki lifted a black device. "Under a blizzard."

Was that a remote control?

"This is gonna be double-double nice-nice," Brattany said, getting ready to hit the record button.

Kiki glanced around at all of the fans in the art room. Six

of them, the big industrial kind, had been spread around, each pointing toward the center.

Each pointing toward us.

Suddenly I saw a sense of organization in everything. Trays of uncovered paint had been positioned in front of the fans on the left. Tubs of glitter, their tops removed, sat in front of the fans on the right. I saw feathers and strips of felt and confetti and sparkly things galore, all placed in a position where the wind from the fans would be sure to hit them.

No wonder it had taken the ThreePees three days to set this up. The whole room had been booby-trapped!

"Don't do it, Kiki," I warned.

"Too late, skinny-chubby...It's done."

Kiki pressed the ON button, and the fans whirred to life.

"Take cover!" I yelled, as if I were in the army. "INCOMING!"

Beanpole and Q didn't budge, because they had no idea what I was talking about.

Seconds later, paint began to fly, splattering everywhere. Feathers and glitter and felt strips swirled about. Within seconds, we were in the middle of a hurricane.

I tried the door again. Still locked.

I tried to turn off a fan, but couldn't see any buttons on it, because of the ever-increasing typhoon of arts and crafts.

Finally, all I could do was try my best to block my face as art materials showered us from all angles. Purple, green, yellow, red. It was like being inside the middle of a cyclone.

Then it stopped. Just stopped. Faintly, I heard a voice.

"That's enough, Kiki. That's enough!" It was Sofes. "You said it wouldn't be that bad."

Kiki laughed. "You get that?" she asked Brattany. "'Cause I can turn them back on."

"No, don't," Sofes protested.

Brattany lowered her phone, checked the playback screen, and smiled. "Got it. Got it all." She smirked wickedly, then laughed. "Wonder how many hits this one will have on YouTube?"

"I wonder how long they are going to sit stuck in there before they're discovered," Kiki responded.

Sofes wrinkled her brow. "You mean we're not gonna let them out? What if they supplicate?"

"You mean, suffocate," Kiki said, correcting her.

"Yeah, what if they suffocate?" Sofes repeated.

"There's air in there," Kiki replied. "And fumes, too, I imagine."

Kiki high-fived Brattany and hooted, "Double-double nice-nice." With the recent budget cuts, our school had an art teacher on campus only three days a week, and today, Friday, wasn't one of them. That meant that it might not be until after the weekend before we'd be discovered.

I gazed at Q. Paint, feathers, and sparkles decorated her forehead. She looked like she'd been mugged by a gang of preschoolers.

"Well," Sofes said, clearly uncomfortable with the idea of abandoning us in a locked room, "what if they starve to death?"

Kiki glanced at us. "I'm sure the porky one will eat the other two before that happens. Now, come on, let's go before someone comes."

"But wait," Sofes protested. "We can't just leave them in there."

"Oh, yes, we can," Kiki shot back. "And we will."

Sofes didn't challenge her further.

"Hey, nerds, we'll leave the key in the lock for you," Kiki said, dangling a set of silver keys in the window where we could see them. "All you have to do to get out is get out to unlock the door and then you can get out."

"Like Houdini," Brattany said as she high-fived Kiki one more time, their payback for what had happened to them at the talent show complete.

Each of the ThreePees took one final look at us from the window. Kiki stared like a military general, as if she were a battlefield commander who had just done some stern and serious damage to her enemy. Brattany wore the smile of a snob, the kind of smirk that belongs to a kid who thinks she's better than everyone else and likes rubbing their noses in it. Sofes, however, bit her bottom lip and twirled a strand of hair. She looked worried, concerned. For her, this was a prank that had gone too far.

"Come on," Kiki said. "We are outee." A moment later, their heads dipped down below the window frame and they were gone, out of sight.

I turned to Q. "You okay?"

Slowly, she reached for her inhaler.

Wheee-bubble-bubble-grrp. Wheee-bubble-bubble-grrp.

"How 'bout you, Beanpole?"

Beanpole raised her eyes but didn't speak. Hurt, betrayal, and disbelief filled her face. I stared for a sec, completely unable to imagine how long a bath it was going to take to get all the paint and glitter off her body. This was what happened when you let bygones be bygones, I thought. People mowed you down.

"We need to get out of here," I said, trying the door handle again.

Still locked.

Beanpole lifted her phone to make a call. She pushed a few buttons, then stopped.

"Ruined." She looked at her device, which had been drenched in paint. "Totally destroyed."

Q and I quickly checked our cellies. "Great, no bars."

"I just wanted to bury the hatchet," Beanpole explained, half apologizing to us, half trying to figure it out for herself. A tear filled with glitter fell from one eye. "I just thought that we should, you know, all try to get along."

I didn't answer. I knew things could never be good between girls like them and girls like us. Meanness was in their blood. And stupidity was clearly in ours.

The only sound in the supply room came from Q.

Wheee-bubble-bubble-grrp. Wheee-bubble-bubble-grrp.

One hour and forty-five minutes later, as we sat stranded in the art room, a *click* broke the silence.

"What the stuffings happened to you?"

Vice Principal Stone, a tall, gray-haired, medium-bellied old guy in a bright red tie, walked through the door.

Of course, we Nerd Girls are a lot of things, but one thing we are not is snitches.

"Nothing," I said, a fuzzy pink feather drooping from my chin.

Neither Beanpole nor Q said a word.

Mr. Stone stared, semi-astounded at the sight of us. He

waited for more of an explanation. We didn't give him one. A gap of silence followed.

Finally, seeing that he wasn't getting anywhere with us, Mr. Stone shifted the black walkie-talkie he was carrying from his left hand to his right, and noticed that Beanpole was holding a cell phone.

"Why didn't you call someone?"

Beanpole lifted her phone. "Destroyed." She was so sad I thought we were going to have to have a funeral for this thing, like it was some sort of fluffy pet that had died or something.

"No bars," I commented, lifting up my phone.

The vice principal tried to assess the situation. Mr. Stone was one of those old-time guys who had been around this school for, like, thirty years, and I could tell by the look on his face that he almost wished he'd never opened that door.

After rubbing his temples in an *I already have a migraine from this* way, the VP slowly raised his walkie-talkie to his lips.

"Stone to office. Stone to office. Copy."

No answer. The VP rolled his eyes and tried again.

"Stone to office. Stone to office. Copy." Mr. Stone gazed around the room. He had to have been thinking, What a disaster.

"You realize I'm less than one year away from retirement, right? I mean, I don't need this," he said. "I don't need this at all."

None of us responded.

"Stone to office, Stone to office. Do you copy?!" he repeated, raising his voice. "Oh, come on," he said in frustration to his walkie-talkie.

"Um, how'd you find us?" Beanpole asked, a Popsicle stick dangling in her hair.

"Anonymous tip," he answered. Suddenly, a voice crackled from the radio.

"Copy, Mr. Stone. G'head."

"Finally," he said before speaking into the radio transmitter. "I need a hose, some soap, and three top-to-bottom Aardvark outfits from the PE room sent back to the C wing of the campus. Copy."

There was a moment of silence on the other end, as if whoever was listening was struggling to understand the request.

"Uhhh . . . why? Copy."

Mr. Stone glared at the three of us before responding.

"Looks like we got ourselves a little situation with some of our scholars."

"**I** say we kill them. I say we rip off their perfect little noses, pluck out their pretty little eyelashes, and feed their earlobes to the birds," I snarled as we sat in the waiting area out in front of Principal Mazer's office. "And that's just to start!"

"Maybe we should consider turning the other cheek?" Beanpole offered.

I stared in disbelief. "Did you just say, 'Turn the other cheek'?"

"Yeah, you know, like end this now, before it escalates even further."

Beanpole shuffled in her seat and did her best not to get any paint smudges on the brown chair. Even after having been demolished by the ThreePees, she remained thoughtful and considerate. Really, I didn't understand the girl at all.

"The only cheek I'm turning is my butt cheek, so they can pucker up and kiss it! I mean, it is ON now. To-ta-lee ON!" I said.

"Yeah," added Q, with a sinister glint in her eye. "Those witches need to pay."

"Think about your phone, Beanpole," I reasoned. "Think about what they did to your brand-new, innocent, never-harmed-a-hair-on-anybody's-head, defenseless little phone."

Conveniently, she changed the subject. "How're your arms, Alice?"

"Still tingly," Q replied, gazing down at her left elbow. Though we'd taken showers in the girls' locker room—pretty much a nightmarish experience even when you don't have blue paint speckling your armpits—our bodies still had traces of the art blizzard all over them. "Lucky for me they only used acrylic-based materials. If they'd used oil-based paint, it could have been real trouble."

I caught a reflection of myself in the glass of the window behind me.

"Jeez Louise, we look like human Picasso puppets. And . . . *achoo!* I have sparkles in my nostrils."

"Bless you," Beanpole said.

"Ooh, we're gonna get those witches," Q said, flashing her best Wild West gunfighter look. "And I mean good."

Wheee-bubble-bubble-grrp. Wheee-bubble-bubble-grrp.

"That thing still works?" I asked, nodding at her inhaler.

"Far as I can tell," she replied.

I stared for a second. "Open," I said.

Q opened her mouth.

"Yep, just fine. Aside from the fact that your tongue is neon green, I'd say your scuba tank is just hunky-freakin'-dory."

Q stuck out her tongue and struggled to see her reflection in the window behind us.

"Ooh, I'm gonna get those witches," she said. "We are gonna..." Suddenly, she clammed up in midsentence.

I looked up. The ThreePees approached.

Kiki, always in the middle, always up front, stepped forward. "Nice school spirit, ladies," she said to us in a taunting voice. "Love the clothes. But what made you all decide to wear Aardvark PE outfits today?"

Brattany struggled to contain her giggles.

"For your information, we're nerdvarks," Beanpole snapped, as if that were really telling her something.

Kiki paused. "Nerdvarks?" She processed the information.

Oh no, I thought. Where in the world had that come from?

"Ha! That's the most pathetic thing I've ever heard," Kiki said with a laugh.

"We've got to put that in the YouTube title somewhere," Brattany noted. "Nerdvarks...that's brilliant."

"Okay, okay, enough of the chitter-chatter." Mrs. Rumpkin, the roundish, crotchety, looks-kinda-like-a-bulldog school secretary, came over to separate us into two groups before there could be any more hostile interaction. "You girls, over there; you stay here. The principal will be right out."

The ThreePees didn't exactly hustle over to the spot across the way where the secretary had pointed.

"NOW!" Mrs. Rumpkin snapped. "And I don't want any shenanigans, either, you got me?!"

The ThreePees, not daring to push it with Mrs. Rumpkin—few

kids ever did—waggled off to a spot about thirty feet away, on the other side of the office. Mrs. Rumpkin returned to a desk covered with papers and yellow sticky notes and all sorts of school memo things, and scowled, defying either group to interact so she could go all bulldog crazy on us.

None of us risked it. Besides, we'd all be in the principal's office soon enough. Forgetting the ThreePees for a moment, I turned to Beanpole.

"Nerdvarks?" I said. "Why would you give them that kind of ammunition?"

"Because," Beanpole said as she sat up tall and with pride, "I'm not ashamed to be a nerdvark." Just then, she realized she was sitting beside a water fountain. Deciding to take a drink, she bowed her head, leaned over, and pressed the button with grace and dignity.

A huge stream of water blasted her in the face. Slowly, she turned back to me, her nose, chin, and cheeks dripping wet.

"We've already talked about this," she continued, as if nothing out of the ordinary had happened, even though water droplets were hanging from her nose. "We've just got to come to terms with the fact that we are who we are." And then, to drive her point home, Beanpole once again straightened her spine and attempted to take the drink she had been unable to take a moment prior.

She leaned forward, pressed the button, and *splash!* got blasted by a huge stream of water for a second time.

She turned to us with a face so wet it looked as if she'd been bobbing for apples.

"I think it's broken."

"Nawww," I said. "Ya think?"

Q pulled a few tissues out of her belt holster—why she was wearing that thing on her PE shorts, I had no idea—and handed them to Beanpole.

"Thank you," Beanpole said as she blotted her face dry. However, when Kleenex gets wet, it sort of sticks to your skin, and a moment later, Beanpole looked up at me with all sorts of white tissue dots stuck to her face.

"What?" she said. "Why are you staring at me like that?"

"You realize that you will never have a boyfriend if you keep this up, right? I mean, unless you have a growth spurt and sprout breasts the size of beach balls, you might as well start shopping for cats."

Beanpole turned to Q. "Is it that bad?"

"Cat pee is my kryptonite," Q replied.

Just as Q began picking white fuzz off Beanpole's mug, Principal Mazer threw his door open and took a long, hard look at us.

What a sight we must have been. Loaner PE clothes that didn't fit well. Spots of half-washed-off paint and sparkles all over our bodies. One of us with a face that was peppered with dots and dashes of white tissue. And, of course, on the other side of the room sat the ThreePees, perfectly coifed and attired.

Principal Mazer pointed. His message was loud and clear. "Inside. Now!"

Heads down, we marched in, the ThreePees following behind us. Mr. Stone, the vice principal, was already inside, sitting in a worn chair in the corner, clearly annoyed that he had gotten caught up in all this nonsense.

"Ladies," Principal Mazer said, taking a seat behind his big wooden meant-to-scare-the-crud-out-of-kids CEO-style desk, "it's time we had a little chat."

"But I'm not even sure why we're here," Kiki replied in her best *I'm an innocent little angel* voice.

"Let's not play games, Miss Masters," the principal said.

"But really," Brattany commented, "we have no idea why we're even in this office right now."

"Yeah," Sofes added. "Like, when they were locked in the art room for the accidental art tornado, we, like, totally have an abibli."

Kiki hung her head in an *I can't believe she just said that* way.

"You mean, an alibi?" Principal Mazer responded.

"Uh-huh," Sofes said, her ponytail bouncing up and down. "One that's rock solid."

"I'm sure it is, Miss O'Reilly. I am sure it is."

Kiki shot Sofes a look filled with laser beams. Sofes shrugged as if to say, *What'd I do?*

"Now, this little competition/rivalry thing has gotten out of hand." Principal Mazer set his hands on his desk, interlacing his fingers. "And I want it to stop."

"But..." Kiki said.

"Removing eyebrows, painting bodies," Principal Mazer continued, without allowing Kiki to finish her thought. "I want this to cease, you understand? NOW!" Principal Mazer is a firm, short man. Not Oompa Loompa short, but short enough so that he is pretty much always the shortest adult in the room. "The pranks. The games. The competition. No more! This ends now, or else."

"Or else what?" Brattany asked.

"Or else," Principal Mazer replied in a menacing tone. "PPWB."

Each of us looked around at the others.

"What's that?"

"Trust me, ladies, you do not want to know." He rose from his chair, a stern frown covering his face. "I am going to have to pay two custodians overtime to deal with that mess, not to mention the cost of the supplies. And with our school budget the way it is, I mean, I ought to just..." He paused and took a moment to compose himself. "Look, kids make mistakes. I get that," he said. "They deserve second chances, too, and I like to consider myself a fair man. But this ends now; am I clear, ladies? No more."

None of us responded. Mr. Stone glared at us from the corner of the room, silent but highly agitated. I could tell that if he had been in charge, we would have been paying a much heavier price.

"I said, AM I CLEAR?!"

"Yes," "Uh-huh," "Clear," we replied.

"Then out!" he ordered. "Before I lose my temper and change my mind."

"But we have an abibli," Sofes interjected, trying to stick to the original game plan she had clearly cooked up with the Three-Pees prior to being summoned to the office. Principal Mazer glared. "I mean, alibi," she said, softly correcting herself.

"I'm warning you, I come from the school of positive discipline, but if I have to take this to the next level, I will. And trust me, nobody will be happy if I do." Principal Mazer pointed toward the door, our time with him done.

The six of us walked out of the office, past the secretary, and left the building. The final period would be ending soon—there were only, like, two minutes left in the day, so there was no need for us to return to class.

However, there was a need to huddle up and scheme. We knew it. The ThreePees gathered on the left side of the infamous Grover Park fountain, and me and my wolf pack huddled up on the right.

"Our next grenade has to be big," I said.

"Nuclear," Q insisted.

"I like how you're thinking," I said.

When the final bell rang, we exited the campus and walked to my house, mapping out our plan for revenge.

"It's gonna have to be one for the history books," I said.

"Hey, since he helped us before, maybe we could ask your brother, Marty, to make their telephones explode?" Q suggested. "Like when they answer a call, *BOOM!* Exploding brains."

"You might have something there," I told her. "Not sure about the death thing, but permanent maiming sounds entirely reasonable."

Beanpole shot me a look, yet remained silent, her lack of words expressing all we needed to know about her feelings on the matter. She's one of those hippie-dippy types, a kid who believes in things like peace over conflict. But look where that had gotten us. If today had taught us one thing, it was that you just can't make nice-nice with dragons.

"Maybe we could go with toenail removal or facial scars?" Q said. "Or tooth chipping, like down to the nerve? I mean, orthodontic pain is always a good one."

"You kind of have a cruel streak, don't you?" I said.

"What can I say?" Q replied. "Those witches"—*Wheee-bubble-bubble-grrp. Wheee-bubble-bubble-grrp*—"bring out the best in me."

"Okay, officially, I have to say that I'm not comfortable with all this revenge talk. I mean, where does it end?" asked Beanpole.

"When they're pulverized," I replied. "See, what we need," I said as I unlocked my front door, "is some good old-fashioned—"

I froze. Stopped. Went ice cold.

There was a voice.

"Hi, dimps, long time no see."

My stomach flipped, and I went white as a swirl of vanilla frozen yogurt. Beanpole turned to Q and mouthed the words "Who's that?"

Q shrugged. "Dunno."

My mom approached.

"Hey, Boo," she said in a warm, comforting tone. "You remember your father, don't you?"

Beanpole's and Q's jaws dropped. They began whispering.

"Her father?"

"But didn't he run out on them years ago?"

I stared blankly.

"Girls," my mom said to Beanpole and Q, opening the door, "can you maybe give us a few minutes, please?"

"Um, sure, Mrs. Saunders," Beanpole said, taking Q by the arm and leading her away. "Come on, Alice. Uh, let's go."

A moment later, the door closed softly behind them. Beanpole and Q decided to head home, leaving me with my parents.

hank God for Saturdays. No school. No teachers. No ThreePees.

Of course, there was still YouTube with its newly posted "Nerdvarks in an Art Blizzard" video for all the world to see. But thankfully, all the world didn't feel like seeing it.

Brattany's Internet attempt to humiliate us didn't catch on. Fact is, it's hard to make a video go viral on YouTube. I mean, there's just so much stuff out there already, and people add even more kooky stuff every day, so it's impossible to know what will become YouTubally popular. Sure, the ThreePees were able to get a whole mess of views the last time they humiliated me at school, but this time their paint tornado video didn't score many views at all. Only fifty-four people had seen it. And I'm sure that at least ten of those clicks were me and Beanpole and Q trying to watch ourselves to discover what had really happened when we were caught in the art-i-cane.

"I think we're going to be safe from international moron celebrity status," I said, turning away from the desktop computer in Beanpole's bedroom. "It's not getting many clicks at all."

Beanpole's house was, to say the least, a unique environment. Once inside, I'd always felt, I dunno, uncomfortably comfortable. Like, too cozy. Maybe it was the snowy white carpet? Maybe it was all the ergonomic furniture? Maybe it was because Beanpole's mother was some kind of Martha Stewart loony bird on interior-design steroids?

Actually, Beanpole's mother is cool. But I did nickname her Department Store Mom, because she always does everything in a way that seems department-store perfect. She sews sweaters from yarn balls, stitches her own curtains, and the food she prepares is like stuff you'd see on the Cooking Channel. Really, to walk into Beanpole's house is to walk into a home where there is always a glass of chilled lemonade, always the fragrance of a scented bathroom soap, and always the love of a supportive parent ready with a kind, warm, understanding smile.

The house is like ice cream: on the one hand, it's the best dessert ever, but on the other hand, when you have too much of it, the sweetness just makes you want to puke.

"But why would he come back now?" Beanpole asked.

I knew it was only a matter of time before she began nagging me about my father.

"I don't know," I said.

"And why would your mother let him in?" Beanpole asked.

"I don't know," I replied.

"And what do you think he wants?" she continued.

"I don't know," I answered.

"And where has he been?"

"I don't know. I don't know. I don't know," I replied. "Now, can you stop asking me so many questions?"

"Well, I could stop asking you so many questions if you could start giving me some honest answers, now, couldn't I, Mo?" Beanpole crossed her arms and stared at me like she had just made a really good point. "I mean, weren't you the one talking about how we should be honest with each other, anyway?"

"Was that another question?"

"Depends on what you mean by the word *question*," she answered. "Technically, I think it was a statement."

"And technically, I think your brain is a roll of toilet paper."

I wasn't trying to be a grumped-out crank, but *jeez Louise*, back off already. Couldn't she tell I was freaked out about the whole thing? I mean, I hadn't seen the guy since before first grade, and now it's like, "Oh, by the way, your long-lost dad is back, let's all bake a pie together." The whole thing made me feel like no matter how much I breathed in, I could never really get a lungful of air, and when I get like that, I don't want to talk about it; I just want to coat my tongue with cupcake batter and pretend none of it is really happening.

Q stared at me.

"And what fantasmical comment about this whole situation might you have to offer?" Arms crossed, I waited for a reply.

Slowly, she raised her inhaler and took a slurp. "Bugs Bunny was"—*Wheeesh-whooosh. Wheeesh-whooosh*—"a wascally wabbit."

"I see," I said, nodding my head. "And oh, look, you fixed your scuba tank," I remarked. Q's portable deep-sea diving unit was now functioning quite properly again. "Tell me, was the trip to Planet Freakwad to get new parts a fast one, or was their traffic?"

"Aardvark."

"Her mom had a spare inhaler," Beanpole explained. "And did I tell you? Good news! Mommy said she would replace my phone. What'd your mom say about your new pants being ruined?"

I didn't respond.

"You didn't tell her what happened, did you, Mo?" Beanpole asked.

"Well... other things were going down."

"Oh yeah, like, what other things were going down?" Beanpole inquired, making yet another attempt to get me to spill my guts.

"Hmm, let's see," I answered. "Some cookies went down. A slice of cheesecake went down. Oh yeah, and a double-scoop banana split with rainbow-colored sprinkles went down, too. Extra whipped cream, of course."

"*Hmmpft*," Beanpole said, shaking her head. Seeing that she was getting nowhere with me, she crossed the room and began looking through her closet.

Some kids arrange their sweaters by style. Beanpole arranges them by the temperature outside. For every eight degrees, the thickness of the fabric as calculated against the estimated provision of warmth determined the hanger color on which the item would rest.

For example, if it was going to be anywhere between sixty to sixty-eight degrees outside, the clothing options hung on green hangers. If the temperature was to drop to fifty-nine degrees, the clothing options rested on navy blue. And so on and so on and so on.

From Jamaican sunshine to polar winters, Beanpole had a color-coded hanger for every type of weather circumstance known on earth. And for each season, she'd rotate her closet so that the most likely clothing needs would be closest to the entrance of her closet door. One day she even hoped to be featured in *Out of the Closet* magazine.

I didn't have the heart to tell her that *Out of the Closet* magazine was a homosexual publication.

"Mo, I think you're thinking with your amygdala," Beanpole said as she rifled through some pullovers.

"My what?"

"The emotional part of your brain instead of the logical part. I read in a magazine about how this happens all the time to kids our age," she answered. "'Cause if you were thinking with the logical part of your brain, you'd recognize that it's logical for friends to share secrets so they can work out their issues."

"I'm not hiding any secrets," I said.

"Hider."

"I'm not hiding."

"Issue avoider."

"I'm not an issue avoider."

"Are too, are too, are too," Beanpole said, with all the maturity of a fourth grader.

I turned to Q. "Would you please talk to her?"

"Wascally," she said. "Very wascally."

I sighed. "Okay," I said. "He did say one thing."

"I knew it," Beanpole replied, shooting out of the closet. "I just knew it."

"He said he wants to fill some holes."

"Fill some holes?" Beanpole asked.

"Yeah, fill some holes," I said. "He says he has a lot of holes to fill."

Beanpole thought about it for a moment. "What does that even mean?"

"Have I yet to mention the words *I don't know* anywhere in this conversation?"

"Sheesh, it's like pulling teeth with you, Mo," Beanpole said, heading back to her closet. Perhaps a tank top had mistakenly wandered into the arctic apparel section or something. "You're so, I don't know ... bottled up."

"I'm not bottled up."

"You're ketchup."

"I'm not ketchup."

"You're worse than ketchup," Beanpole said. "You're like restaurant ketchup with the burger getting cold and nothing coming out of the bottle as the french fries get soggy."

"Ketchup makes my eyelids twitch," Q said, informing us of yet another fascinating factoid. "But whole-grain mustard is a good source of omega-3."

"I'll start a blog," I replied.

"All right, all right, I have an idea," Beanpole said, jumping onto the bed for some girl-chat time. "Clearly, you'd feel more comfortable if I shared some secrets with you first, so I'll tell you something about me to get us started, okay?"

"Not okay."

"It'll be fun."

"I don't want to hear your secrets, Beanpole."

"I never poop at school."

"What?!"

"Neither do I," said Q.

"Yeah," Beanpole confirmed. "Like, even if I have to go really bad, I hold it until I get home. Just something about the idea of making a school doody that gives me the creepies."

"I'm afraid of toilet water," Q confessed.

"You're afraid of toilet water?" Beanpole asked, wrinkling her nose. "Like, what about at your house?"

"We put those little thingies in the tank to turn the water blue," she explained. "Calms my colonic nerves."

"Has it ever occurred to either of you that some secrets are meant to be kept to yourself?" I asked.

"Also, sometimes," Beanpole continued, apparently feeling as if we were really getting somewhere now, "instead of clipping my toenails, I bite off the edges."

"You chew your own pedicure?" I asked.

"I'm pretty limber," she answered. "Wanna see?"

"Not really."

Too late. Before I could say another word, off came Beanpole's shoe.

"You know, you really don't have to—"

Beanpole swung her leg around to demonstrate how she could nibble her toenails, but in her zeal she accidentally knocked over a giant pink alarm clock, which fell directly on her foot.

"Ouch!" she exclaimed. The clock lay sideways on the floor, going *beep, beep, beep.* "Don't worry, don't worry, I'm okay."

"Am I karmically paying for some kind of past-life debt right now?" I asked of no one in particular.

"You should give him a chance," Q said. The room went silent. "I mean, he is your dad."

I stared. Q stared back. I stared some more.

"Oh, great," I said. "No guilt there."

"I'm just saying," Q answered.

The three of us sat quietly, each of us lost in her own thoughts. Why couldn't things be simple again, like when I was in first grade? When you're seven years old, life's biggest problems are all about toys and candy and bedtime. When you're thirteen, they're all about, well...everything.

"Is there any way we can get back to plotting the devastation and destruction of the ThreePees?" I asked. "I mean, isn't that why we're here?"

"Maybe we should use ketchup." Beanpole suggested, a ton of sarcasm in her voice. "The restaurant kind." With a disapproving look, she reentered her closet, grabbed a pair of navy blue high-tops, and placed them inside an empty cardboard box that sat beside her dresser.

Then she did it with a pair of black leather moccasins. And then a pair of one-inch heels. I gazed at her with a *What are you doing with all those shoes?* look on my face.

"For donation," she explained.

"They look brand new."

"They are."

"Yet each a different size," Q commented, as if she were observing a practically invisible mustard stain on the tie of the real murderer in a Sherlock Holmes mystery.

I wrinkled my brow. "Huh? What are you talking about?"

"One's a size seven and a half, one's a size nine," Q answered, as if she were saying, *Elementary, my dear Watson.*

"Really?" I crossed over to the box and pulled out two brown open-toed sandals. They were two different sizes.

"How'd you know that?" I asked.

"Aardvark."

Wow, so observant. I lifted up a pair of green-and-white tennis sneakers that had just been placed by Beanpole inside the box. "Why is each of these a different size?"

"Because I have two different size feet, silly." Beanpole reached into her closet and held up the matching pair of green-and-white tennies. "I keep these and I donate those. Gets expensive, but my orthopedist thinks this is why I'm so clumsy. My feet are growing at different rates."

"That's weird," I said.

"Not really," Beanpole answered. "A lot of kids have one foot that's bigger than the other."

"It's still weird," I said, putting the sneakers back inside the box.

"Could be worse," Beanpole said. "Some girls have boobs that grow at different rates. Imagine bra shopping for that."

Different size knockers? I looked down at my chest and realized I had better keep my mouth shut before I angered the Gods of Breastness and ended up with a watermelon on one side of my rib cage and a tangerine on the other.

"This is why I'm going to take tai chi," Beanpole informed us.

"Tai what?"

"Tai chi. It's this ancient Chinese exercise martial-arts thing that uses slow movements. It'll help me with my balance." Beanpole slowly spread her arms wide and smiled. "I'm gonna be one with the universe."

Placing her palms together in front of her chest, she closed her eyes and began to chant. "*Ommmmm.*"

I turned to Q. "Is she serious?"

"I wonder if they'll ever make a crayon color called Spinach. Don't you think the world would be a better place with spinach-colored crayons?"

"Do you ever answer the question you've been asked?" I said.

"Beetlegunk."

I decided it would be silly to continue the conversation with Q. This was her way of having fun with me; the more frustrated I grew, the more entertained she became, and this time I wasn't falling for it. Thank goodness Beanpole finally opened her eyes.

"You know, I've been reading up. With tai chi I will learn to accept the universe as it is."

"I thought you said it was a martial art," I replied.

"I don't really know what it is. My first class is next week," Beanpole answered. "Maybe I'll learn some karate too, like, *Hi-ya!*" she exclaimed as she jumped into a fighting stance.

Unfortunately, Beanpole hadn't looked behind her when she exploded into her martial-arts display, and her back arm smashed into a stack of medium-weight sweaters. Quickly trying to catch them before they fell, she surged forward but tripped over her uneven size feet...which caused her to bonk her head into a hanger, knock over eight pairs of blue jeans, lose her balance entirely, and fall head over heels into the Windbreaker section of her closet, the area that had been reserved for moderate gusts.

I let out a deep sigh as clothing items designed for inclement weather collapsed on her head.

"Don't worry, don't worry, I'm okay." She emerged from the closet, a wool sock dangling from her ponytail. "I'm okay."

Clearly, there was a tai chi teacher somewhere who had no idea what she was about to get into.

Back at school on Monday, the plan was to try to get the ThreePees to eat some "complimentary peppermints" that would have caused their teeth to turn green and red. My brother was great with pranks and stuff like that—the fake wrappers made these breath fresheners look like the real deal—but Kiki and her two ding-a-lings didn't fall for it, and they avoided catastrophe. Not sure what happened to the mints, though. They mysteriously disappeared after we left them on the lunch counter.

On Tuesday, I was almost fooled into eating a chocolate-chip cookie made with horse laxative, which most probably would have sat me on the toilet for a week. However, at the last minute, I was warned about them by Logan Meyers, the blond-haired, blue-eyed Greek god of middle-school boys.

"Hey, Maureen," Logan whispered, just before the bell rang

to dismiss us from social studies. "They did something to some cookies today."

"They did?" I said nervously, knowing exactly who he was talking about. "Thanks," I told him.

"Don't mention it," he replied with a bright white smile. "Besides, when you really think about it, cookies are stupid."

Earlier in the year, I admit, I'd had a HUGE crush on Logan. But after we did this project together for Mr. Piddles's class, where Logan made, like, four hundred fart jokes while I did all the work, I began to see that a girl should like a boy for more than just his looks, even if he is hot like a jalapeño pepper.

"I mean, I'm more of a video-game guy myself," Logan continued, as if he hadn't already told me this about a zillion times. "Video games are not stupid."

"Yeah, well, thanks, Logan. You really saved me."

"I mean, even the *stupid* video games are not stupid, you know?" he said.

"Indeed," I said, closing my notebook, looking for a way to end the conversation.

"Like, this stupid school doesn't stupid-appreciate how not stupid video games are. Am I right or am I right or what?" he argued.

"Preach it, brutha. Preach it," I said, hoping that if I agreed with him he'd let the whole thing go.

"Thank you," he said, happy to see that there was at least one person who could really understand where he was coming from (even though I had no idea where he was coming from).

Logan wandered away. As he did so, one thought, one inescapable, unavoidable, never-to-be-disputed fact, filled my brain.

He's got a cute butt.

I blame genetic programming for random zone-outs like this.

After I managed to avoid Tuesday's booby-trapped cookies, Wednesday and Thursday were free of pranks, but when lunchtime came on Friday, it was Game On once again.

Q's eyes darted from side to side, looking around to make sure no one was watching us. The outdoor courtyard, where we always ate lunch, bustled with activity. Boys punched other boys, then ran off. Girls played with their phones while gossiping or doing homework. A few kids flirted. Nothing out of the ordinary, just another Friday on campus. Once Q felt the coast was clear, she reached into her backpack.

"I got the goods right here," she whispered.

I cranked my neck to see what she'd brought.

"Exploding pens. The kind that, when you press down to write, they will"—*Wheeesh-whooosh. Wheeesh-whooosh*—"blast a squirt of ink into the person's face."

"Niiiice!" I said.

"I got them at the magic store down on Harris Street," Q continued. "But how are we going to get them into the ThreePees' hands?"

"Good question," I said as I gazed across the courtyard. Just as we were huddled around the table trying to come up with a way to really stick it to the ThreePees, it seemed they were also huddling to try and figure out a way to stick it to us.

"Can I just officially say that I don't like any of this?" Beanpole remarked. "I don't like it at all. I mean, every time I sit at a desk I check for tacks or 'Kick Me!' signs or glue. It's making me crazy."

"Hey, glue," I said. "Good idea, Beanpole."

"Yeah," said Q, her eyes glowing with possibilities. "Maybe we could glue the witches to a park bench, cover them in corn kernels, spread maple syrup over their faces, and import some Australian crows to eat out their eyeballs!"

"They've wounded you, haven't they?" I asked.

"More than you know," Q replied.

"How come I don't think you two are really listening to me?" Beanpole asked.

"We're totally listening, Beanpole," I said, getting ready to ignore her again. "Just go play with your phone or something, while we figure this out."

"I'm not getting it till this weekend," she said. "By the way, have you heard from your dad again?"

I pretended not to hear the question. "So, the ink that will be squirted, is it blue?" I asked Q in regards to the magic pens.

"Deep purple," she answered. "Think grape juice."

"Niiice," I said.

"You know, Mo," Beanpole said, knowing that I'd quite clearly heard her question yet chosen to ignore it, "denying reality doesn't change reality."

"Well, if God didn't want me sweeping reality under the rug, then why did he make me so good with a broom? Now," I said to Q, "what if we put the pens—"

Suddenly, Mrs. Chambliss, one of the vice principals, walked up to our lunch table. She was wearing a yellow sweater over a white blouse with a necklace made of topaz. While some teachers are slobs who look like they don't even own an iron, Mrs. Chambliss always dresses with class and style.

"All right, girls...let's go."

"Where? Why? We didn't do anything," we protested.

"Tell that to the principal," she responded. Like all vice principals, Mrs. Chambliss held a black walkie-talkie in her hand, and used the antenna to point out the direction in which we needed to go. "Now, move."

Across the courtyard, Mr. Piddles, the social studies teacher who did double duty as lunchtime monitor, approached the ThreePees and started pointing toward the front office as well. A moment later, they were on the march.

Kiki and I made eye contact across the courtyard, both of us knowing we were headed to the exact same place: Principal Mazer's office.

Well, bring it on, I thought. Bring it on.

The six of us didn't make a peep as we entered the principal's office. Vice Principal Stone was in the room, wearing a striped tie—purple and black—that did not quite match his light peach shirt. He glared from the left-hand corner, looking even more hostile and uptight than usual.

"Did I not tell you that I wanted this to stop? Didn't I?!" growled Principal Mazer.

"But..." Brattany said in protest, "we didn't do anything."

"Oh, yeah?" Principal Mazer barked. "Then how come Mr. Stone looks like he swallowed one of Santa's elves?"

Mr. Stone flashed his teeth. They were green and red and frightening.

"*Eeek!*" I yelped.

"Plus," Principal Mazer continued, "the poor man's had

diarrhea for the past seventy-two hours. Does anyone care to explain what kind of poop potion you put in those cookies?" He glared, practically with steam coming out of his ears. When Oompa Loompas get mad, watch out.

"They did it!" Kiki shouted, pointing at us.

"Huh? What? We did not," I replied. "You did it!"

"No, you did!"

"You did!"

"All right, ENOUGH!" Principal Mazer said. "You wanted it, you got it. You are now the official PPWBs of Grover Park Middle School."

There was a moment of confused silence.

"The what?" I said.

"The PPWBs," Principal Mazer said. "The Personal Polishing Worker Bees." He rose from his chair. "You're going to polish basketballs. You're going to polish tubas. You're going to polish doorknobs and desks and toilet-flushing handles and gum-stained carpets."

"Um, how do you polish a gum-stained carpet?" Brattany asked.

"On your knees," Mr. Stone said, with menace in his eyes. "On your knees."

I gulped. Boy, those teeth were scary. And they completely clashed with his tie, too.

"But, honest to goodness, we didn't do anything," Kiki said in her best *I'm a little angel* voice. She even fluttered her eyelashes.

Barf, I thought.

"Save it, Miss Masters," the principal said. "I like to think I am a man who keeps his cool and finds productive ways to reach his students, but you girls, well...Just maybe this will polish some dadgum sense into your heads."

There was a knock at the door.

"Sorry to bother you, sir, but I just need a quick signature to approve the Academic Septathlon flyer," Principal Mazer's secretary said.

"Come in, Mrs. Rumpkin, we're just finishing up here anyway," the principal told her.

"But isn't there some way we can avoid the PPWB, or whatever you call it?" Kiki asked as the secretary passed a sheet of paper to Principal Mazer.

"Yeah, polishing isn't good for my polish," Brattany said, holding up her fingernails as if to present her manicure to the court as official evidence.

"Sure..." Principal Mazer replied absentmindedly as he signed the sheet of paper. "Win the Academic Septathlon and all is forgiven," he said in an offhand way.

"Fine, we'll do that," Kiki said.

"No, *we'll* do that," I shot back, not wanting to give an inch.

"No, we will."

"We will!"

"Stop! Nobody is going to do that," Principal Mazer explained. "I mean, sure, I'd like to think someone from this school could win it, but Saint Dianne's has won it nine out of the past ten years, and the last seven in a row. Heck, we haven't even been able to field a Septathlon team for the past two or three years. Students have just totally lost interest."

"We'll do it for you, sir," Kiki said, straightening her spine like the world's biggest suck-up. "We'll carry the torch of school pride."

The torch of school pride? OMG, so pathetic.

"No, *we* will carry the torch of school pride," I insisted. "And we will carry it to the educational summit of Mount Olympus!"

Hey, no one's going to out-suck-up me.

"No, we will!"

"We will!"

"Just be quiet a minute!" Principal Mazer ordered, covering his ears. "Holy goodness, what is with all of you?"

He stared at the flyer, considering how to proceed.

"Okay, here's what I'll do," he said, some kind of positive-discipline lightbulb going off in his head. "We'll have a little qualification tournament. The team that earns the right to represent our school will have their PPWB time cut in half. And if you win and beat Saint Dianne's, you're off the hook entirely."

"And the team that loses?" Brattany asked.

"Polishes," he replied. "Polishes until I can see my smile in every door handle on this campus, no ifs, ands, or buts. Is it a deal, ladies?"

Kiki looked over at her two pet Chihuahuas.

"Deal," she said.

"Deal," I replied, without a moment's thought, not giving the ThreePees an inch. Beanpole practically bounced out of her seat with excitement. Considering that she was the type of girl who actually liked homework, the thought of an Academic Septathlon totally wound her dorkasaurus clock. Q, on the other hand, showed a glint of Wild West gunslinger in her eyes. In the battle of brains, there was no one coming to the table with more gray matter than her.

"The Septathlon is in four weeks. Our qualification tournament will be a week from Monday," the principal explained.

"Ten days?" I exclaimed. "That's not enough time." Being that I had already participated in Math-a-thon a few years ago, I knew exactly how much work it would take to get prepared for this sort of thing. Science, history, music, language arts, these Septathlon things were no joke.

"I have toilet-paper-roll dispensers that could use some buffing right now if you prefer, Miss Saunders," Principal Mazer said. "And let me ask, have you ever been in the boys' bathroom on the first floor? The smell alone can turn your nose hair green."

I recoiled in horror.

"No, ten days is great, sir. Easily done."

"Here are some study materials to get you started," the principal said, opening up a closet. A moment later, each of us was holding a binder. Not just any binder, of course, but the biggest binder of intellectual materials ever put together. They must have been the size of two phone books, weighing twelve pounds each. I mean, brain surgeons probably need to know less to remove cranial tumors.

"Wait," Sofes said to Kiki. "Do we, like, have to learn this, or do we just carry it around for show, like we do with all our other schoolbooks?"

Kiki ignored her.

"Good luck, ladies," Principal Mazer said. My arms practically sank to the floor with the weight of the tome. "I love that Aardvark spirit."

In the corner of the room, Mr. Stone glared. Clearly, he wanted us to start polishing—and I'm sure buffing out his Christmas teeth was at the top of the list.

"By the way, girls," Principal Mazer added, "if there is one more prank between now and the contest—and I don't care who does it—the deal is off. Am I clear?"

"Clear," we said in low voices.

"I said, AM I CLEAR?" Principal Mazer was one hundred percent serious. "It's time for a truce, you hear? If you want to compete with one another, you'll do it in a positive, productive manner. Now, out."

The six of us trudged out of the principal's office carrying a rain forest's worth of paper.

Goodness, hadn't these Septathlon people ever heard of deforestation?

After carrying the entire academic history of recorded human knowledge to our last two classes, Beanpole, Q, and I met up at our usual spot, next to the fountain by the front gate.

"This is going to be so much fun!" Beanpole said, shifting the cinder-block-size binder from her left hand to her right. "I mean, just think of the . . . *OUCH!*"

She dropped earth's database on her foot.

"Don't worry, don't worry, I'm okay," she said, bending over to pick up the zillion-pound binder. "Just a small bump."

BAM! Beanpole smashed her head into the cement ledge of the fountain. Her legs wobbled, and for a second I wondered whether or not she was going to remain conscious.

"You okay, Barbara?" Q asked. It sounded like Beanpole had fractured her skull.

"Ouch-a-doozie," Beanpole said, her palm covering her

forehead. "Did it leave a mark?" She moved her hand so I could see the damage.

Yeesh! It looked like she'd been struck by a meteor.

"Nah," I said. "Can hardly notice."

"Good," she answered, rubbing her noggin. "'Cause nothing's going to stop me from learning every piece of information in this entire book. When do we start?"

"We don't."

Both nerdwads stared at me.

"What do you mean, we don't?"

I looked out into the parking lot, where a bunch of parents were picking up their kids in the carpool loop. Students screamed, a few couples held hands (ahh, teen love . . . *barf!*), and some car horns honked.

"You heard me; we don't," I repeated.

"But how are we going to win the qualification tournament if we don't study?" Beanpole asked, not quite understanding.

"Do you know how much time it's going to take to prepare for the Academic Septathlon?" I replied. "We would have to stay after school five days a week to get ready. Plus, meet on Saturdays. Plus, on Sundays. It would swallow our entire existence."

"But you're the one who volunteered us," Q said.

She had a point. But that's because I was thinking with my abee-dah-bee at the time, or whatever that thing was that Beanpole had called it—the emotional, not logical, part of my brain. Really, I just didn't want Kiki to get the better of me, that's all. And when I get all riled up like that, I'm like an annoyed rhinoceros. I don't use my head; I just get all passionate and thoughtless, and stupidly charge forward without thinking things through.

"I got caught up in the heat of the moment," I confessed in an *I made a mistake* tone. "But trust me, no one *wants* to do the Academic Septathlon. I mean, why do you think our school hasn't been able to put a team together for years? It takes up too much time and you have no life."

"I already have no life," Beanpole said.

"Me, neither," Q agreed.

"Well, I do," I told them. "Granted, it's pathetic, but still, I don't want to spend every waking moment of my day until Thanksgiving break learning school stuff like a nerd."

"But you are a nerd," Beanpole said.

"This is nerd squared," I said. "No, scratch that. This is nerd cubed. No, wait...This is nerd to the power of nerd times nerd!"

I readjusted my backpack. The beastly Septathlon binder didn't fit all the way inside. I couldn't even zip the stupid zipper.

"Polishing cleansers cause my quadriceps to cramp."

"Don't worry," I said to Q. "By next week I'm sure he'll have forgotten all about this polishing nonsense."

Neither Q nor Beanpole was buying it.

"Okay, so we'll have to wipe down a few whiteboards, maybe mop a floor," I said. "Big deal; it won't be that bad."

"So we're just going to let the ThreePees win?" Q asked.

"There is no winning," I said. "I mean, sure, we could easily trounce those witches, but whoever goes to the city championship is going to get slaughtered by those private-school girls, anyway. They've got coaches and experience and all that. The only thing we'd really win is a chance to lose by a zillion points and get publicly humiliated on a big stage in front of a whole lot of people."

"Nice optimism," Beanpole said.

"Just saving us the embarrassment," I replied. After all, my entire life was about embarrassment. It was smart to play defense, to cut stuff like this off at the pass before it eventually blew up in my face. If I'd learned anything by this point, I'd learned this much: stay away from situations that hold the potential for gigantic public humiliation. Could there be an easier rule to follow?

The three of us stood in uncomfortable silence as a car horn blared in the distance. *Beep-beep.*

"Are you serious, Mo?" Beanpole finally said. "I mean, are we really not going to do this?"

"We have to make 'em pay *nerrrd style*," Q said in her most intimidating voice.

Beanpole and Q nodded in solidarity and then decided to high-five each other.

But missed.

The momentum of fanning on the high five sent Beanpole tumbling into a flower bed. She quickly popped back up, soil in her hair.

"Don't worry, don't worry, I'm okay."

"I'm just going to pretend I, like, didn't see that," I told them. *Beep-beep. Beep-beep.*

"Look," I continued, "I want to thrash the ThreePees more than anyone, but I just don't want to end up spending all my time studying every subject under the sun, knowing that no matter what I do I still have no chance to—" *Beep-beep.* "*Jeez Louise,*" I said, after yet another car-horn honk. "What moron has the parent who keeps blasting away on their stupid horn?"

"Um, you do, Mo."

"What?"

"Look," Beanpole said, pointing toward the carpool loop. "It's your father."

My father?

I spun around. It was my father. He got out of the car and waved at me.

He was wearing an untucked white dress shirt rolled up at the sleeves, blue jeans, a large watch, and midlife man sneakers, the kind you can't actually run in but are made to look sporty (if you are a midlife man, that is). His mostly brown hair had relaxed curls in front, but some gray streaks at his temples showed he wasn't a spring chicken anymore. However, his face was still kind of boyish. I thought I looked nothing like him.

"You kinda look like him," Beanpole said.

"Stuff a piece of pita bread in it, doof face."

He waved again.

"He's picking you up?" Q asked.

"Uh, I guess. Must be part of his whole 'holes to fill' thing." I didn't move toward the vehicle.

"How's your"—*Wheeesh-whooosh. Wheeesh-whooosh*—"brother taking it?" Q inquired.

"Marty?" I said. "He's like a silent volcano. Totally ignores him and looks as if he's ready to explode at any moment."

"And Ashley?" Beanpole asked.

"He gave her twenty bucks yesterday. She thinks having a dad is cool."

My father waved a third time. Why had mom given him her car? I wondered.

"And what about you, Mo?" Beanpole asked. "How are you doing with it all?"

"Well, let's see . . . My divorced mom is now re-dating my re-divorced dad," I said as my father blocked the flow of traffic and cars began piling up behind him. I mean, everyone knew that the carpool loop was a no-waiting zone.

Yet still, there he was, waiting.

"What's a re-divorced dad?" Q asked.

"He got married and divorced after he married and divorced my mom," I explained. "Thus, re-divorced."

"And you never told us any of this?" Beanpole said, looking at me with big ol' bug eyes. "Oh, you are so ketchup."

I stared at my mom's car. I didn't want to go over there. And I certainly didn't want to share a car ride home with my long-lost father so we could fill some stupid holes, whatever that meant.

"This is just so, I dunno . . . weird-o-rama," I said.

My father, smiling, waved a fourth time.

I half waved and half smiled back. Feeling encouraged, he motioned to me with his arm, as if to say, *Come on. Get in.*

"So, what are you gonna do?" Beanpole asked.

"Eat something fudgey."

"No, seriously, Mo. What are you going to do?"

"Why would you think I'm not serious about that?" I took a deep breath. "Well . . . I guess I'm just gonna have to go over there and tell him the truth."

"The truth?" Beanpole said in a surprised voice. "You mean, like about how emotionally conflicted you are with him so suddenly trying to re-enter your life?"

"No, of course not," I said, as if that were the dumbest thing

I'd ever heard. "I'm gonna tell him how busy my schedule is going to be, due to all the time I'll be spending on the Academic Septathlon."

Beanpole stared at me in disbelief.

"Heck, if we go all the way to the national finals, I might not be free until Christmas vacation of the year 2086."

Each of them looked at me in amazement. Q spoke first.

Well, sort of.

Wheeesh-whooosh. Wheeesh-whooosh.

"Oh, don't start with me, cheese brain," I said, understanding every word she had meant, by the tone of that last scuba dive. "I haven't had enough doughnuts today to deal with this."

"Mo, I've just got one word for you," Beanpole said, in a calm voice.

"Oh, yeah, what's that, Beanpole?" I asked.

"Restaurant ketchup."

"That's two words," I said.

"Clogged up as you are, what's the difference?" she replied. "Do you want me to go with you?" she asked. "Like, walk over for support?"

"Naw, thanks," I said as I headed toward the car. "Just wait here. This should only take a sec."

"Okay, here's the deal," I said to Beanpole and Q as we got ready to roll on our first study session. We'd decided to study at Beanpole's house, because Q's mom would have been helicoptering over her daughter way too much for us to get any real work done, always wanting to make sure she felt good, wasn't pushing herself too hard, blah-blah-blah. And my house was out, because Superdad might unexpectedly pop in wanting to go on some kind of hole-filling, daddy-daughter, let's-reconnect, bonding excursion at any moment. And oh, what a joy that would have been. If I wasn't careful, I might have found myself standing in some grassy park flying a plastic kite.

Pah-thetic.

"'The Academic Septathlon,'" I read to my fellow nerdsters from the introduction in the binder, "'is a seven-subject competition in Art, Music, Science, Math, Language, Literature, and

History.'" I looked up. "And let's not kid ourselves. This thing's a monster."

Beanpole and Q nodded.

"How about we see where we are with a few practice questions first?" I asked.

"Ready!" said Beanpole, bubbling with perkiness.

"Q, we'll start with you," I said. "The category is Science."

I randomly turned to page 524 and began reading from the study guide:

"Which one of the following processes can occur only in a living cell?
a. bulk filtration
b. endocytosis
c. osmosis
d. diffusion
e. molecular protein expulsion"

Teen Einstein would have struggled with some of these brain-benders.

I raised my eyes and waited for an answer.

Silence.

I waited some more.

More silence.

Q rubbed her chin, thinking.

I waited some more.

And some more and some more and some more.

Finally, Q opened her mouth.

Wheeesh-whooosh. Wheeesh-whooosh.

"Okay, let's flip to another subject," I said, trying to be encouraging. "The category is Art."

I randomly chose a question from page 921:

"The printing process in which ink is forced into recessed lines is called:
a. lithography
b. intaglio
c. collograph
d. woodblock printing
e. screen inkage"

I raised my eyes and waited for an answer.
Silence.
I waited some more.
More silence.
I waited some more and some more and some more.
Wheeesh-whooosh. Wheeesh-whooosh.
"All right, Beanpole. Let's try you."

"Hit me!" Beanpole rubbed her hands together, studious and intent.

I flipped to page 678. "Let's go back to Science. That's always a biggie in competitions like these anyway.

"Humans and chimpanzees share a common ancestor. If you compared their genomes, you could determine:
a. why humans have vestigial structures
b. what atavistic stepping stones led to humanity

c. which species developed first

d. which species is most evolved

e. how long ago the populations separated"

"May I have a definition, please?"

"Excuse me?" I said.

"I'd like a definition, please."

"You can't ask for a definition, Beanpole." I turned to Q. "Can she ask for a definition?"

Q shrugged. "They do in spelling bees."

"But this isn't a spelling bee, this is the Academic Septathlon. Check the rules."

Q turned to the rules section of the 906,268-page binder.

"There are one hundred fourteen pages of rules, and it's all written in lawyerese," she said, leafing through the pages. "Hmm, interesting."

What to do? I thought.

"You can't have a definition, Beanpole."

"I'd like a definition."

"But you can't have a definition," I said.

"And how do you know that?" Beanpole asked.

I hesitated.

"See, you don't," she snapped. "And unless there's a rule saying that I can't have a definition," Beanpole argued, "I think it's only fair that you give me a definition."

I turned to Q. "Did you find it yet?"

She began reading.

" 'For international contestants competing on domestic soil, the Academic Septathlon will be given in English, but in the event that the competition is being'"—*Wheeesh-whooosh. Wheeesh-whooosh*—"'given in a country other than an English-speaking nation, the contestant will have the option of'"—*Wheeesh-whooosh. Wheeesh-whooosh*—"'taking the test in the country's native language.'"

"Why would you read me that?" I asked.

"Operational functions intrigue me," she answered.

I took a deep breath, struggling to keep my composure. "Just answer the question, Beanpole."

"Can you repeat it, please?"

I glared.

"What? You asked it a long time ago," she said, in her own defense. "I don't remember what it was."

I slowly looked down at my binder. "The category is Science. . . .

**"Humans and chimpanzees share a common ancestor.
If you compared their genomes, you could determine:**
a. why humans have vestigial structures
b. what atavistic stepping stones led to humanity
c. which species developed first
d. which species is most evolved
e. how long ago the populations separated"

"I'd like a definition."

"You can't have a definition."

"How do you know?"

"I don't," I said.

"So why are you acting like you do?" she asked.

The two of us turned to Q, looking for her to settle this disagreement once and for all. She read from the rules. "'Inquiries regarding borderline course subjects should be referred to the State Director, who will make the'"—*Wheeesh-whooosh. Wheeesh-whooosh*—"'determination of eligibility based on the academic nature of any questionable course of suitable study.'"

"Well, thank you for that," I said. "Your entirely irrelevant point is duly noted. Now, Beanpole…" I turned my attention back to her so that we could get some actual studying done that day. "Let's just say I am able to provide you with a definition. Being that I do not even see a dictionary in your room, where would I get this definition from?"

"From our phones, of course," she answered, holding up her new cellie. "We'll use our phones to go online. Don't you just love your phone, Maureen?"

"I'll tell you where I'd love to stick my phone," I muttered. I turned to Q. "Do the rules say that we are allowed to use our cell phones during the competition?"

She began to read.

"'In the case of a non-neutral match site where there is no recognized arbiter for disagreements, a coach'"—*Wheeesh-whooosh. Wheeesh-whooosh*—"'reserves the right to challenge any irregularities in the proceedings.'"

"Well, that certainly seems to answer it, now, doesn't it?"

"I think I'm gonna read all the rules," Q informed us. "You never know when you might need 'em."

"You do that," I said. "Matter of fact, maybe one day you

can even rise to the grand height of becoming a Middle School Rule Referee. And wow, wouldn't that be something to tell the grandkids?"

Beanpole stared at me, her hands on her hips, waiting for a definition. "Well..."

"Okay," I said in an exasperated voice as I reached for my phone. "I mean, we haven't even covered one stupid question yet, but all right, I'll start surfing the Web for a definition for you." I prepared to go online. "What word do you want a definition for?"

"I forgot. Can you repeat the question, please?"

"'In the event of environmental disruption, competition shall resume from the point of play at which'"—*Wheeesh-whooosh*. *Wheeesh-whooosh*—"'the contest was halted, unless circumstances prevent a re-continuation of the match.'"

I calmly closed the ten-thousand-pound book sitting in my lap.

"So you're not going to reread the question?" Beanpole asked.

"No, I am not going to reread the question," I said. "And I am not going to listen to subsection B, paragraph 11, bullet points 7, 8, and 9 as to why I should, either. Instead," I said, raising my cell phone, "I am going to go online to learn all that I can."

"About the Academic Septathlon?" Beanpole asked.

"No," I replied. "About the disposal of human body parts!" I slammed down the book, waved my arms, and started pulling at my hair. "AAAAAARRRGGHHH!" I screamed. "*YEEEEESH!* Sometimes the two of you make me so nuts."

Q stared, calm and serene.

"You're funny. Do that again."

Suddenly, there was a knock at the door, a knock that probably saved one of those two from being force-fed a study binder.

"Who's ready for a snacky-wacky?"

It was Department Store Mom. She was wearing a green apron with a matching green hair bow and a crew-neck white sweater. Beanpole's mom whirled into the bedroom as bubbly as a can of Pepsi being poured over ice.

"Snack? Oh, am I ever ready, Mrs. Tanner!" I said, practically salivating at the sight of the homemade goodies she carried on her silver tray. "After all, it's a scientifically proven fact that ingesting large amounts of sugary foods is a great way to reduce stress."

"*Mmmmm*," I said. "Gingerbread. And are these chocolate-hazelnut? Wow."

She had made two types of snacks today. Probably one batch was for Q, made entirely from ingredients that wouldn't trigger any sort of allergic reaction, since she couldn't have nuts. Pistachios, almonds, hazelnuts, peanuts—especially peanuts—were off-limits for her.

I looked over the creations. Before I ate any of Department Store Mom's food, I always had to take a moment to appreciate the artistry. She was like some sort of cooking van Gogh, except she still had both her ears.

Today's nibblers had been made in the image of a girl fiendishly wringing her hands together, plotting dastardly revenge. Between the homemade white icing, the black-and-red sprinkles, and the use of slivered raisins for eyes, it was clear that Department Store Mom had spent a heck of a lot of time bringing these cookies to life.

"You really went all out today, Mrs. Tanner," I said, reluctant to even take a bite because they were so beautiful.

But I did. *Chomp!*

"Mess with my kid and it's game on, Maureen."

"Game on is right, Mrs. Tanner," I assured her as I chewed up the head of little Miss Ginger Vengeance. "We're gonna get 'em good."

"Yeah," Q said. "Get those witches good. Wait till you see what we have in store for them."

"But I thought we were going to uphold the truce," Beanpole said, alarmed by the news.

"We are," I answered. "Until we aren't, of course," I added with a smile. Q and I had been kicking a few ideas around behind Beanpole's back. No need to bring Miss Goody Two-shoes into the conversation until our plan was better formed, we decided.

Q squinted like a gunfighter and then reached for a cookie.

"Oh, Alice, dear, the cookies on the left are for you," Department Store Mom said, pointing to the treats she'd made with Alice in mind. "The ones on the right have nuts in them."

"Oh," Alice said softly.

"We could just make friends with them, you know?" Beanpole offered.

"I'd rather drink paint," I answered. "Oh, wait, I already did that." I munched the head off a second cookie. "Besides, I bet you they're preparing to get us right now, anyway."

Q nodded in agreement.

"But where does it end?" Beanpole asked.

"Hopefully, with them groveling and begging for our

never-to-come mercy," I answered. "At least, that seems like a good start."

"My tai chi teacher says that we need to be one with the universe, accepting it as it is," Beanpole informed us, "and be peaceful within it."

"Are we seriously going to take the advice of a person who wears pajamas to work?" I asked.

"It's called a *gi*," Beanpole answered. "They're not pajamas."

"Getting along would be best, of course," Department Store Mom said as she straightened an already straight picture frame on the wall. "However, if you're expecting the meanness toward you girls to simply stop on its own, well...that may be a bit naive, honey. Sometimes you have to stand up for yourself in this world."

Beanpole's father popped his head into the room. He was wearing a checkered sweater and tan khaki pants, like he had just stepped out of a commercial to promote the grand opening of a new shopping mall.

"Come on, honey," he said to his wife. "We don't want to be late for the grand opening of the new shopping mall."

Sometimes being with this family was like entering the Twilight Zone.

"Oh, hey there, girls," Department Store Dad said to Q and me. "Hey, sporto, you guys going to be okay if we go out for a while?"

"Sure thing, Daddy," Beanpole answered.

"Is there a sale on sweaters, Mr. Tanner?" I asked.

"One can only hope, Maureen," he replied with a smile. "Now, don't have too much fun without us, okay, girls?"

"There's lemonade, mint tea, and pomegranate juice in the fridge if you get thirsty," Department Store Mom said as she got ready to depart. "And there's apple cider and with-pulp as well as pulpless orange juice, too," she added. "But if you decide you want a coffee drink, I whipped up a batch of decaf iced cappuccinos and chocolate mocha lattes, although we're running low on maraschino cherries, so there might not be enough for a second round of those if you decide to go for a refill. As for water, we have bottled flat, bottled sparkling, distilled flat, distilled sparkling, lemon flavored, raspberry, kiwi, lime, mixed berry, or no-salt seltzer. Are you sure you girls are going to be okay? We'll be gone a few hours."

"Well, there's a potential they'll drown," Department Store Dad said with a chuckle. "Come on, honey, they'll be fine. Besides, my juices are all revved up thinking about cardigans. What's got your engines revved today?"

"Doilies," she answered. "I am all about the doilies this afternoon."

Like lovebirds from an old movie, Department Store Dad and Department Store Mom left arm in arm, headed for the new mall.

"See, even your mom wants us to blast them," I noted after they'd gone.

"That's not what she said, Mo," Beanpole said. "And how come no one told me about any 'plans' we have to get them again?"

"In due time, Beanpole," I said. "For now, you can relax, 'cause we're just going to lie low and lull them to sleep."

"Yeah," Q said mischievously. "Lull 'em *nerrrd style*." She reached for a cookie.

"WAIT!" Beanpole screamed.

I jumped back. "What?"

"Don't eat those, Alice. They have nuts," Beanpole said, coming to Q's rescue.

"I know," Q answered calmly. "It's okay." She picked up a chocolate-hazelnut cookie.

It's okay? Beanpole and I cocked our heads to one side. *What did she mean by that?*

"I'm seeing a new doctor," Q explained. "He thinks my allergies are psychosomatic."

"Psychosomatic?" Beanpole asked. "What's that mean?"

"It means she's psycho," I said. Q glared. "Sorry . . . Go on."

"My doctor thinks that by exposing myself to things I think I am allergic to, I can build up an immunity and prove to myself that I am really *not* allergic to the things I think I am allergic to."

I took a moment to try to figure out what all that meant.

"And this is a licensed doctor?"

"Would you let her finish, Mo?" Beanpole said. "She's trying a new form of treatment. I think that's nice."

"Instead of avoidance, she recommends exposure," Q informed us.

"Wait a minute—*she*?" I replied. "A second ago you said it was a *he*."

"She's a team," Q said. "I mean, they're a team. It's experimental. If I can beat my allergies, then my mom can stop worrying about me so much and get her life back. She used to have a career and everything, you know." Q looked at the cookie. "And since nuts are the biggest problem for most kids like me who have allergies, I'm going to start here."

The room fell quiet as Q stood eye to eye with her arch-allergic enemy, the nut family.

"Well if you ask me—" I began.

"Which nobody did," Beanpole interjected.

"But if you did ask me," I continued, "these docs sounds like quack-quack ducks. I mean, how is someone who is allergic to something going to become nonallergic to something just like that? Don't they know the reactions you have?"

Beanpole glared.

"I'm not trying to be a hater," I explained. "I'm just worried about her, that's all."

Q studied the chocolate-hazelnut cookie she held in her hand. Simply touching the thing could cause her issues, but eating them?

"I'm doing it for my mom. I have to get better for her. She's already sacrificed way too much for me."

"G'head, Alice," Beanpole said. "Eat one. I support you."

Q eyed the treat.

"And Mo supports you, too," Beanpole said, nudging me. "Don't you, Mo?"

They both looked at me, Beanpole seeking to encourage my support, Q with an expression that showed she was nervous and really, really needed to have me in her corner on this one.

"I support you," I said. "Even if your head explodes and mushy gray juice oozes out of your ear hole, I support you."

Q raised the chocolate-hazelnut cookie to her lips.

"My doctor thinks my brain is sending the wrong signals to my body and can be retrained," she said, hoisting the cookie into the air as if she were making a toast. "So, here's to new brain signals."

"And to health insurance," I added.

Beanpole elbowed me. "We support you, Alice. Even if we have a funny way of showing it."

There was a pause, just like when a kid is standing at the edge of a really tall diving board wondering whether to jump or turn around and climb back down the ladder and put their feet safely back on the deck.

"Focus on how great it'll be once you're free from these things," Beanpole said. "I bet you'll be cured in no time. Trust the science."

Slowly, carefully, Alice took a bite of the chocolate-hazelnut cookie.

"Yep, just trust the science," I conceded.

Though there was a slight breeze, it was warm on campus, the sun shining, the sky blue, the cover over the outdoor lunch tables providing just the right amount of shade. Days like today were the reason people loved California so much, especially when there were reports of snowstorms and hail on the East Coast. The only thing I knew about snow was that you weren't supposed to eat the yellow stuff.

I think that was a pee joke.

"Clear the way!" I cried. "Hubcap ears, coming through!"

"Don't make fun of her like that, Mo," Beanpole said as we sat down at our regular lunch table toward the back of the courtyard. "You know she's sensitive."

"But it's Monday, and her ears are still the size of coconuts," I replied. "What'd your doctors say?" I asked as Q sat down on the bench across from me.

"Skunk stink can only be washed off with tomato juice."

She began to unpack her lunch.

"Huh?"

"Skunk stink can only be washed off with tomato juice," she repeated.

"What's that even mean?" I asked.

"It means," she said, "that sometimes you need to endure some yuck in order to get to where you want to go. And I know exactly where I want to go." She looked at me with fierce determination. "I'm going to help my mom."

Without a doubt, Q was the most stubborn person I'd ever met. If she set a goal, she accomplished it; that was that. I watched as she set her lunch items on the table.

Today's midday cuisine for Q consisted of seedless watermelon, a few slices of roasted, no-salt turkey, a couple of crackers, and a Ziploc bag filled with peanuts.

Peanuts? She couldn't have been serious. But just as I was about to question the wisdom of her eating them, my cell phone buzzed. I checked the screen to see who it was, pushed a button, then tossed the phone into my backpack and reconsidered having any sort of chat with Q about her being nuts to be eating nuts. After all, she was gonna do what she was gonna do, so I decided instead to focus on my own heart-healthy midday meal: a plate of cafeteria nachos and a king-size bag of Flamin' Hot Cheetos.

Okay, perhaps Cheetos weren't the most nutritional item on the menu, but when I read the back label on the bag, I did see that they were made with enriched cornmeal, and that's gotta be some kind of vegetable, doesn't it?

"Was that a text?" Beanpole asked me.

"Yup," I said. Truth be told, there is nothing like the experience of that first Flamin' Hot Cheeto scorching your tongue. What a burn! I mean, there is no way to describe it to someone who has never been through this fiery taste-bud pleasure dome before.

"Who was it from?" Beanpole asked. Her lunch was a vegetable frittata that had been crafted into the Torch of Academic Wisdom. I guess Department Store Mom was hoping that if Beanpole ate the scholarly symbol for brains, some of it would rub off.

"My dad," I replied, as the sting of the Flamin' Hots began to make my eyes water. The way those Cheetos could tie pleasure with pain together in my mouth deserved some sort of award. "My mom gave him my school schedule, so now he knows things like that my lunchtime starts at eleven thirty-eight, and stuff like that."

"Hole-filling?" Q asked.

"Exactly," I answered, my tongue ablaze. Good thing I had the nachos to put out the inferno. A few bites of corn chips—see, there's vegetables once again—smothered under a glop of cheese pumped from a jar was just the thing I needed.

Of course, eating lunch like this is a science, and I'd never recommend it to amateurs. Or adults. A person could get seriously injured if they didn't know exactly how to handle the various hazardous food materials I was juggling in my oral cavity. Ask any kid: tongue fires, singed stomach linings, roasted gum lines—they've all been known to happen with this flavor of Cheetos. When they say Flamin' Hot, they're not joking around. This chip bag needed a warning label on it.

"Sooooo..." Beanpole said.

"So, what?" I said, licking the red plutonium dust off my fingertips.

"What do you mean, 'So, what?'" Beanpole said. "So how'd you respond to your dad's text?"

"Two words," I told her. "Dee. Leet."

"Well, here's two words for you, Mo," she said in a momly voice. "Ketch. Up."

Why couldn't Beanpole just mind her own business? I mean, here she was with a sweater-wearing father whose biggest thrill in life was cardigan shopping at the new mall, and yet she felt like she was entitled to pry, pry, pry, as if she could just...

"Uh-oh..." Q suddenly said, gazing across the courtyard. "We've got company."

I dropped my train of thought and spun around. Marching toward us were the ThreePees.

"Did you arrange this?" I asked Beanpole sharply.

"Nope. Swear," she replied.

The ThreePees jiggled closer.

"Whaddya"—*Wheeesh-whooosh. Wheeesh-whooosh*—"think they want?"

"I'm sure it's just to play mind games with us," I said. "That's what they always try to do. So, look, whatever you do," I instructed, "don't engage with them. Especially on an emotional level. No passion. No argumentation. No nothing but calm, even-tempered logic. In order to win the Academic Septathlon, we have to practice remaining cool under pressure."

The ThreePees were almost upon us.

"Nothing but ice. Got me, ladies? Nothing. But. Ice."

The ThreePees wiggled up to our table wearing spaghetti-strap tops and funky, rainbow-swirl flip-flops. When it came to fashion, they always had the latest, freshest clothing.

Kiki spoke first. "You do realize we're going to thump you, right, dork heads?"

"Oh, yeah?" I barked, leaping out of my seat. "Well, I've got some news for you, Keek-o-la. We've been putting in mad, crazy hours of study, so get outta of my face unless you want a piece of this right now. Do ya?! Do ya?!"

I was so riled up Beanpole had to jump in front of me.

"Accept the universe, Mo. Accept the universe."

Note to self: consider reducing the amount of caffeine in diet.

"Oh, yeah, think you're so smart?" Brattany taunted. "What's the capital of New York?"

"The city or the state?" Beanpole replied with a *You're not going to fool me* look on her face.

Uh-oh. Had to think. Quick!

"Who invented the Pythagorean theorem?" I shot back.

"Don't even go there," Kiki said dismissively. "Mr. Theorem, of course."

Ooh, perhaps they did know something.

"What's the square root of pi?"

"Apple or pecan?"

"How many metric meters are in a gallon?"

"A gallon of water or a gallon of lemonade?"

"How many elements are on the periodic table?"

"How many elements are on a buffet table?"

"Is the table wooden or does the table have a marble countertop?"

The questions flew everywhere, each of us trying to outdo the other. And then came this:

"If you've got seventeen office chairs and they are each traveling sixteen miles per hour from the northeast on a train with scheduled stops every quarter mile, how many desks and how many trains will you need if the sun sets in the east on a leap year during a full moon? Huh? How many? How many? Huh?"

Everyone stopped and stared.

"Too challenging?" asked the girl who had just posed the question.

"Sofes, is your headband wrapped too tight?" Kiki shook her head, a look of total disapproval in her expression. "Like, is it cutting off the circulation to your brain?"

"Just stick to the stuff you know, Sofes," Brattany pleaded. "We talked about this."

"You mean like hair?" Sofes replied.

"Like silence," Kiki snapped. "The less you talk, the better."

"Yeah, the better for all of us," Brattany noted.

Sofes's shoulders slumped. "Like, um, just trying to help," she said softly.

"Like, um, you're not," Kiki responded. "So don't."

Suddenly, Mr. Piddles shuffled up, out of breath.

"Is there a problem, ladies?" he asked, stepping between us.

Mr. Piddles was a bald-headed man who wore neckties with short-sleeved shirts, a fashion faux pas if ever there was one. His great mission in life, though, was not clothing trends; it was promoting justice. In fact, he cared more about justice than any person I'd ever known. Heck, those ties he wore? Some of them were Statue of Liberty–themed.

Another fashion faux pas.

"No," Kiki said, her eyes burning as she glared at me. "There's no problem, sir."

"Nope. No problemo at all, Mr. Piddles," I responded, glaring back at Kiki. "Everything is just fine, fine, fine."

Of course, Mr. Piddles wasn't stupid. And he wasn't buying it, either. To him, hostility between groups of kids on campus didn't represent a proper, just, educational environment, and the look on his face made it one hundred percent clear he wanted all of this to stop.

Thankfully, the ThreePees, being that they were on our lunchtime turf, started to back away before Mr. Piddles got some kind of "justice" idea in his head. I'm sure they wanted to avoid having to do something stupid, like give an oral report in social studies on the importance of respecting one's fellow citizens. Mr. Piddles was always trying to teach life lessons that way, and students avoided being punished by him like the plague, because he always made you do things where you actually had to think and weigh and consider stuff in order to get the work done.

"See ya, soon, señoritas," Kiki said sarcastically, getting ready to lead her coven of witches back to the other side of the courtyard.

"You mean we're not even gonna finish our lunch together?" asked Sofes.

"Not you, Sofes! You're coming with us," Kiki said, grabbing her fellow ThreePee by the arm. "I was talking to them."

"Oh, I was wondering," Sofes replied. "Because that would have been different, you know, like, if you had left me over here."

"Trust me," Kiki said, walking away, "a part of me thinks that's where you really belong anyway."

"Yeah, like Nerdville might be your natural habitat," Brattany said, as she inspected her fingernail polish. "*Urrggh*," she added. "If I am going do well at this brainiac competition, there's no doubt I am going to need a mani-pedi."

And with that the three donkeys disappeared back to their own side of the universe.

Mr. Piddles, however, continued to scowl. Clearly, he didn't like any of it, and I could see the little teacher wheels spinning inside his head.

With another look at me—why he was always lasered in on me, I had no idea—to communicate the idea that *There'd better not be any more issues*, Mr. Piddles returned to his lunchtime monitoring station, where I'm sure he was engrossed in something fascinating like reading the U.S. Constitution in its original longhand form.

When the three of us were alone again, Q spoke in her Wild West gunslinger voice. "Yeah, see ya soon, señorita. See ya real soon."

"Sheesh," I said. "The way we're going, we might as well rename it the Academic Stinkathlon. We still have *so* much to learn."

"Don't worry, Mo," Beanpole said in a perky voice. "We're nerds, and nerds always do great at this kind of stuff."

"Quick," I said, pulling a pop quiz on Beanpole in order to sharpen her skills. "What's the fifth planet from the sun?"

"May I have a definition, please?"

"You want a definition for the word *planet*?" I asked.

"It's within my rights."

"But it's a word you already know," I pointed out.

"Yes, but how do I know that the word I know is really the word I think I know?" she asked.

"Beanpole, I have no idea what you're talking about." I turned to Q. "Have you figured out whether or not this is within her rights yet?"

Q opened her study binder. "'A satisfactory grade point average ensures eligibility in the competition, which will be calculated though'"—*Wheeesh-whooosh. Wheeesh-whooosh*—"'the agreed-upon standards set forth by the mandates in the official guide.'"

"Tell me," I asked, "have you read anything other than the rules, to prepare?"

She didn't respond.

"You haven't, have you?"

"What can I say? I'm attracted to regulatory procedures."

"OMG, we are toast," I said. "Toast with butter and jelly and fancy marmalade on top."

Q looked at her binder, turned the page, and scanned the text.

"'The eating of food during competition is expressly forbidden unless medical reasons preclude'"—*Wheeesh-whooosh. Wheeesh-whooosh*—"'such an exclusion.'"

She paused. I stared, with menace in my eyes.

She continued. "'Subsection F says that a doctor's note, if on hand, will prevent disqualification, should any contestant need to recuse themselves from participation, and a'"—*Wheeesh-whooosh. Wheeesh-whooosh*—"'substitute, the next contestant in the scheduled order of appearance, shall be required to assume the role.'"

"WHY ARE YOU EXPLAINING ALL THIS TO ME?" I yelled.

"You mentioned toast."

"Have I also mentioned ax murdering?"

Q smiled. A moment later, Beanpole looked up from her phone.

"I found it!"

"Found what?" I asked.

"The definition. Online." She silently read the screen of her phone. "Yep, okay, I now know what a planet is."

"You now know what a planet is? Like, didn't they cover that on *Sesame Street*?"

"What I mean is that I now know that what I thought I knew is what I really now do know," she replied.

Sure, there was plenty of stuff in that last sentence that would have given me ample justification for jamming a few printed pages from the study guide down Beanpole's esophagus, but we had a competition to get ready for, so I simply went along with it.

"Okay, Beanpole," I said, heaving a sigh. "So what's the answer?"

"Can you repeat the question, please? I forgot what you asked."

My cheeks started turning as red as a Flamin' Hot Cheeto.

"You're funny, like cartoons," Q said as she picked up a peanut.

"Please tell me you are not going to eat that," I said.

"Aardvark."

"If her doctors say it's okay, she has to trust the science," Beanpole replied. She slowly began to wave her arms in the air like she was moving her hands through invisible water. "Be one with the peanut."

"Be one with the peanut?" I said. "That's your advice?"

Beanpole stood on one foot, waving her limbs. "We are all one with the peanuts of the universe. *Ommmmmm.*"

"Here goes nothing," Q said, hoisting the lumpy tan shell. "Down the hatch."

A part of me wanted to reach out and take all the nuts from her and eat them myself, so that I wouldn't have had to watch her immune system do a "Call the paramedics!" hula dance for us right then and there. On the other hand, if I prevented her from eating those peanuts, there were plenty more in the world, and she just would have gotten another batch for herself later.

Really, what could I do but sit back and watch the fireworks?

Q popped the peanut into her mouth and began to chew. Beanpole and I stared, waiting for her nose to melt or her liver to catch fire or something like that, but nothing happened. Nothing at all. Q just chewed and chewed with no visible effects whatsoever.

"You do know that you're not supposed to eat the shell, right?

She stopped crunching. "You're not?" She thought about it for a moment. And then started crunching again. "Oh, well. Adds an interesting texture."

"Be one with the peanut," Beanpole said, waving her arms. "Accept the universe's peanuts the way they are."

I swear, both of them were cuckoo. Yet nothing happened. Q ate her whole bag of peanuts, shells and all, and made it through the rest of the day without so much as a sneeze. And Beanpole, with her two different size feet, had reduced the tripping, falling, and bonking by about a millionfold.

Maybe there was hope for the two of them. Of course, our real war was yet to come.

10

For the next four nights, the three of us turned up the study heat. I mean, sure, at first I really didn't want to put in the gigantic effort, but once I realized how great it would be to entirely whomp the crud out of the ThreePees, I became an aca-dorkic learning machine. And my NFFs were right there with me. Beanpole, Q, and I met after school each day from 4:15 to 10:00 p.m., just cramming and cramming and cramming away.

I was also cramming cupcakes, but hey, as all athletes know, carbs equal energy.

The thing about all the cramming was, it worked. Well, kinda. What I mean is that we started to get better. Of course we couldn't learn everything there was to know about the Septathlon in eight days' time—not even close—but after hearing test question after test question, we not only absorbed a bunch of material, but our instincts began to sharpen, as if we could feel which answers were wrong and which answers were right.

Basically, the practice sessions took us from being entirely abysmal to being mediumly bad, a significant improvement, considering where we had started.

To be fair to our moms, since they had to make dinner for the three of us and drive us home at the end of the night, we'd decided to rotate houses for each of our sessions. Beanpole's house was ideal because it came with a full catering staff, and Q's house was tough because Q's mom was always coming in to make sure her hemoglobins weren't break-dancing; and on Wednesday night, I would have done anything to avoid its being my house's turn.

There was just no escaping it.

Of course, my fellow dorkmeisters had been to my house lots of times, but not since the long-lost hole-filler had started popping up. Overall, I'd done a good job of avoiding him—not replying to his text messages, coming home late, and so on—but for tonight's study session I needed to make sure I'd have a zero-contact evening with Mister Blast-from-the-Poppa-Past.

Basically, I figured we'd dash up to my room, lock the door, and have my mom slide a pizza under the door when the coast was clear.

"Make sure she sends up ketchup, too," Beanpole said, when I told her the plan. "The restaurant kind."

"Har-har, you're so funny."

When I filled my mom in on how I wanted everything to go, she said it wouldn't be a problem.

"Far as I know, your father isn't even planning on coming over tonight," she said.

"Perfect!" I replied.

Mom furrowed her brow.

"I mean, aw, too bad," I said. Maybe he'd taken off again and I wouldn't next see him till, I don't know . . . college graduation.

The college graduation of my grandchildren, that is. See, some kids, like Beanpole, are always willing to embrace change and give it a chance. Me, I don't like change; I like comfort. I like familiarity. I like leaving my house in the morning and coming home to find it just as it was.

My father represented chaos. He was gone, he had bailed on us long ago, and now he wanted to return? *Let's just keep things the way they are, huh?* I mean, Twinkies didn't just up and change their recipe; why should my dad be able to just up and change his? And if he did, why should I have to just up and change mine? Gooey white cream injected inside spongy yellow tubes of cake, a food formula that worked. If it isn't broke, don't fix it, I say.

"The coast is clear, kiddo." My mother only called me kiddo when she wanted to make a point about something, like when she was trying to say something without really saying it. I hate it when moms do that. I mean, it didn't take a genius to see that she was none too happy about the way I was avoiding my father's reappearance in our lives. In fact, the look on her face made it seem as if she wanted to talk about it, like actually have a heart-to-heart conversation with me at that very moment. So, trying to be respectful of her feelings, I took the lead in handling her not-so-subtle hint.

"Thanks for the pizza. Extra cheese, please. Gotta go, Mom. 'Bye."

I dashed up the stairs, went to my room, and closed the door.

Phew! That was close.

When it comes to sweeping things under the rug, I think I was born with a broom.

Inside my bedroom, Beanpole and Q had already gotten comfortable in their usual spots. Beanpole was relaxing in the semiworn tan seat by the window, her legs crossed yoga style, while Q was sitting—where else?—in the corner of the room, knees up against her chest like a human mouse.

It was time for business, I thought. After all, there weren't that many study hours left until the qualification tournament. I surveyed my team and figured this was as good an opportunity as any for a few inspirational words to fire up the squad.

"You guys stink!" I yelled. "Now, quit slacking off and start showing some effort. And don't cry to me about my plan for all of us to stay up until midnight tonight, either. I am sick and tired of feeling like the mayor of Loserville—population YOU!!"

Focusing on the positive was a quality my mom always tried to instill in me. Clearly, as the leader of my team, I took the importance of always being an optimist to heart.

"Q!" I barked, like an army general readying my troops for battle. "Let's hear the scores of those practice tests we did yesterday, to see how we did."

"Got 'em right here," she said, removing a few pieces of paper from the pocket of her study binder. "Drumroll, please . . . Out of forty questions, I answered . . . twenty-four right."

"That's it, just twenty-four?" I said. "After all that studying we've been doing?"

"You should talk," Q said. " You only answered twenty-one right, and you don't even know any of the rules."

"That's it, just twenty-one?" I hung my head. "I need a plate of doughnuts, a bag of cookies, and a double order of chili-cheese fries."

"What about me? What about me?" Beanpole asked, jumping up and down, excited to think that she could be the winner. Unfortunately, she was sitting underneath a bookshelf.

CRASH! "Ouch!"

A few picture frames, a globe, and all seven of my Harry Potter books came raining down on her head.

"Don't worry, don't worry, I'm okay," Beanpole said.

"You break it, you buy it. Got it, Beanpole?"

"Sorry, Mo," Beanpole said, putting everything back. "Okay, I'm ready for my score. OH, WAIT!" she said, closing her eyes. "Be one with the universe. Ommmm."

"Can we get on with this, please?" I said as she chanted for oneness. "The universe wants us to quit wasting its time."

"I need to be centered," Beanpole replied. "When I get too excited, I lose my sense of oneness and bash into things. Okay, Alice. I'm ready."

"And Barbara's score is . . . twenty-five and a half!"

"Yeah!" exclaimed Beanpole, jumping for joy. Of course she hit the bookshelf again. CRASH!

My picture frames, my globe, and my Harry Potter collection fell on her head once more.

"Don't worry, don't worry, I'm okay."

"I take Visa or MasterCard." I turned to Q. "How in the world can she be the aca-dorkic stud of our team? Let me see those scores." I took the answer sheet from Q and began to look it over. "A twenty-five and a half? How does someone even get a half point on a fill-in-the-blank test, anyway?"

"She wrote in her own answer to question seventeen, and in my opinion," Q said, "it earned a half credit."

"Do the rules even allow for someone to earn a half credit?"

Q opened her binder. "'In case of an emergency, such as a fire, flood, earthquake, or'"—*Wheeesh-whooosh. Wheeesh-whooosh*—"'other natural disasters, the competition will—'"

"Stop, stop, stop," I interrupted. "I don't want to hear about how a plague of locusts will affect the stupid event. Just tell me, what was question seventeen, anyway?"

"Was that the one about who discovered America?" Beanpole asked, recalling the problem that had given her trouble. "Yeah, that question was questionable."

"The question was questionable?" I said. "How was that question questionable?"

"Because it could have been the Native Americans, or it could have been Christopher Columbus, or it could even have been that Amerigo Vespucci guy from Italy who discovered America," Beanpole pointed out.

Wow, I thought. She has been studying.

"So, what'd you put?" I asked.

"Read it; it's right there."

I gazed down and read Beanpole's answer aloud.

"'Can I have a definition of America, please?'"

Beanpole smiled big and wide.

"And you gave her a half credit for that?" I asked Q. "You're not even supposed to write words on these types of tests."

"Aardvark." Q popped a peanut into her mouth and ate it, shell and all.

"You know, I've already thought about what I'd tell the FBI when they start asking questions about your disappearance," I said. "I'm just warning you. I already have an entire plan worked out that—"

"PIZZA!" There was a cry from downstairs. I froze at the sound of the voice.

"Is that..." Beanpole asked, "your father?"

"Come on! Get it while it's hot!"

Yep, that was definitely my father.

"You guys are eating family dinners together now?" Beanpole wondered aloud.

"Um...no," I answered.

Beanpole reached for her backpack. "We'd better go."

"Go?" I said. "You can't go. We have about a thousand hours' worth of work to do."

"We'll start early tomorrow," Beanpole said, gathering up her stuff. "Besides, it's been a long week. I'm tired."

Q reached for her book bag, too.

"You're not going to stay, either?" I asked.

Tears began welling up in my eyes. I was scared, and both of them knew it. But they also knew that giving my father a second chance was something I needed to do, even if I didn't want to listen to them tell me that over and over, each in her own unique way.

"I wonder if peanuts would taste good on steak," Q said. "Or pork. Maybe I'll make a peanut-pork pie tonight."

"You can't avoid him forever, Mo," Beanpole said in a gentle, caring voice. "I mean, even ketchup eventually comes out of the bottle."

"That's not what I was hoping to hear," I said.

"You'll be fine," Beanpole replied. "After all, he's your dad."

I looked at Q. The sadness in her brown eyes said everything. She missed her dad. Terribly. And she would have given anything just to hear him walk through her own front door one more time, shouting, "PIZZA!"

Yet, as we all knew, that would never happen for Q. However, as I had tried to explain to her before, her dad and my dad were not the same dad. She'd the kind of father that a kid would eagerly buy one of those cheesy Father of the Year coffee cups for. Me, I had the kind of dad that made me eager to buy my mom a Mother of the Year coffee cup. Plus, I would give Mom picture frames and balloons and silly little refrigerator magnets, too. That's the kind of dad I had.

"Doesn't matter," Q told me. "You only get one, Mo. In this world, you only get one."

She put her bag of peanuts away. Seeing that there was no way of convincing either of them to stay, I walked them to the front door with a lump in my throat the size of a recliner chair.

"Are you sure you don't want to sleep over?" I asked, making one final attempt to change their minds. "Or better yet, I could sleep at one of your houses. Really, I'd be no bother. I mean, Q, we could just move your Darth Vader machine off to the left and—"

"Go have some pizza, Mo. We're there if you need us," Beanpole said, cutting me off. "But right now, you need us to leave."

Since there was still plenty of light left outside, they decided to walk.

"'Bye," I said, waving like some kid saying, "So long" to his favorite pony as they took it to the glue factory.

"'Bye," Beanpole called out.

"Aardvark." I couldn't tell from where I was standing, but I think Q was crying. "Fourteenth time."

A moment later, they were gone. I took a long, deep breath, turned around, and went inside to join my "family." We met in the dining room. However, I wasn't hungry. And if ever there were a sign that something was wrong with me, I am sure that that was it.

"Yay, Giuseppe's!" my sister Ashley said. Ashley was eleven, had sandy brown hair and a lean, strong physique. Gymnastics was her thing. She loved tumbling and jumping and swinging from stuff, and even though we sometimes fought like birds and squirrels, I had to admit she was pretty good on the balance beam.

"Giuseppe's has the best pizza ever," she exclaimed, grabbing a slice.

"Extra cheese, kind of well done, just like you guys like it," my father said, handing me a slice as if he knew all sorts of precious little fatherly things about me.

Which he didn't.

I was sure my mom had clued him in on the way I liked my pizza. I slowly took the plate and glanced at her. She avoided eye contact with me.

"Come on, Marty," my father said, extending his arm to hand my brother a piece of pizza. "Dig in."

"I'd rather choke."

Marty was skinny, like my sister; not an ounce of fat on

either of them. (They'd saved that gene for me, I guess. Oh joy.) His brown hair, which hadn't seen a comb in months, drooped over his forehead, covering a corner of his silver-framed glasses. However, it didn't interfere with the laserlike glare of hate that was aimed directly at our father.

Silence washed over the room. The tension was thicker than the mozzarella on the pizza pie. My brother stood there defiantly, arms crossed, not budging as my father continued to hold out the plate, waiting for him to take the slice of pizza.

He didn't.

"Okay," Mom said, finally ending the standoff. "Family conference time."

She set down her pizza, took the plate from my dad, and set that one down, too. I felt condor-size butterflies flapping around in my stomach.

I hate family conferences, I thought as I sat down at the brown wooden table. But Marty didn't sit. He continued to stand, his arms crossed, his eyes blazing.

"That means you, mister," Mom ordered, losing her patience with her sixteen-year-old son. Getting angry was pretty rare for Mom. I mean, usually, she was the most tolerant person I knew. "Now!" she demanded.

Marty, realizing he had better not mess with her, uncrossed his arms, pulled out a chair, and turned to his left.

"That would be, a conference for *our family*," Marty said to our father, taking his seat, "as in, NOT including you."

"Marty!" bellowed Mom. "That is not how—"

"No, no," my dad said. "It's okay."

He slowly reached for his coat, which was resting on the back of his chair. "There's a lot of holes to fill," he said. "And some are bigger than others."

"And some are unfillable, *Daaaaad*." Marty spoke with a kind of sarcastic bite I'd never heard out of him before. He had the look of a hive of wasps.

Whoa, does my brother have guts or what? I thought.

My father didn't reply. Instead, he just put on his jacket and quietly walked out of the house. Hadn't touched his pizza, either. Hadn't even said good-bye. Clearly, Marty's words had hurt.

As soon as the front door closed behind him, Marty spun around. "Why are you even seeing him, Mom?" he asked in an accusatory tone. "I don't get it."

"It's just, well...relationships are complicated, honey," she answered. "Me and your father, we have, you know, a history together. And we have you."

Mom looked around the table at each of us and started to get teary.

"And the three of you are the best thing that ever happened to me."

I could see wrinkles at the sides of her eyes, in spite of the cream she used every night. To me, she had always been really pretty, but she was now in her mid-forties, getting older. And a little flabbier, too. Plus, there were a few more brown specks on her hands and arms, like freckles. Those few specks, though, especially for women, add up.

"Well, I think he's cool," Ashley said, offering her two cents. "And he wants to buy me a new computer."

"He's trying to buy your love," Marty said dismissively.

"No," Ashley replied. "He's trying to buy me a new computer.

And you should see the one he's going to get me, Maureen," she said, turning to me. "It's like, totally awesome."

I half smiled.

"You're too young to understand," Marty told her.

"I'm old enough to understand that having a dad who wants to buy me a cool computer is better than not having a dad who wants to buy me a cool computer."

"Whatever," said Marty.

"Whatever to you, monkey butt." Ashley hated being talked to like the baby of the family, even though she was the baby.

"Keep it up and I'm going to feed your tongue to my fighting fish, Ash."

"Just stop it, both of you," Mom said. She turned to me. "What do you think, Boo?"

I stared at the pizza. The urge to eat suddenly returned. Not just a little, either. I felt like eating the whole pizza, box and all.

"I dunno," I answered.

"You don't know what?" Mom asked. Seeing the tears in her eyes made my eyes well up, too.

"Anything," I said. "I don't know anything."

We sat there for a moment, lost in our own thoughts, as the pizza got cold.

"Well, I only have two things to say," Marty declared. "Number one, I don't trust him."

He rose from his chair.

"And number two..." We all looked up. "I never will."

With that, he stormed out of the room.

The next day, as I sat at our usual table, waiting for Beanpole to unfold the day's architectural lunch wonder—it looked like her mom had made something with columns and gargoyles for her to eat—Vice Principal Chambliss, dressed in a forest green pants suit, approached.

"Okay, ladies . . . one more time," she said, using her walkie-talkie antenna to point in the direction of the principal's office.

"But we didn't do anything," I protested. And it was the truth. We really hadn't done anything. Other than work hard preparing for the Academic Septathlon, that is.

That's when it hit me: the ThreePees probably had.

"Tell it to the judge," Mrs. Chambliss said in an unsympathetic voice. "Let's go."

I picked up my backpack and started telling myself there was no way I was going to clean locker-room grime off shower stalls just because those toads had gotten busted trying to stick it to us. I mean, that would have been just so like the ThreePees, too: get caught, lie, snitch on us, then set it up so that we'd be the ones to pay the price while they got away scot-free and laughed all the way to the makeup counter.

Well, no way. My neck tense, my eyes starting to squinch, I marched my way to Principal Mazer's office. By the time we'd arrived, I was in a full stomp.

The ThreePees were already inside.

"I just want to say before you even begin that we didn't do anything," I blurted out. "Not a thing."

Besides the ThreePees and Principal Mazer, Vice Principal Stone and Mr. Piddles were in the office.

"Maureen, no one is..."

"But you don't understand," I interrupted. "We really, really didn't do anything. And it's just not fair, because they keep getting us into trouble even though—"

"*We* get *you* into trouble?" Kiki said, as if that were the most shocking thing she'd ever heard. "All you dorks ever do is talk about us behind our backs and try to figure out ways to—"

"Who are you calling a dork, you snob?" I said.

"Who are you calling a snob, ya nerd?" Brattany replied.

"ENOUGH!" barked Principal Mazer. "Goodness gracious, enough, already." He turned to my social studies teacher. "It seems you are correct, Mr. Piddles. They do not seem to be learning that which is most important in all of this at all. We'll go with your suggestion."

"I do think it's most just," Mr. Piddles replied.

"Uh, what suggestion?" I asked. The six of us exchanged confused looks.

Principal Mazer rose from his desk to make an announcement. "We have a winner," he declared.

"A winner?" Brattany asked. "You mean for the competition?"

"Yay!" Sofes clapped. "I didn't even get any questions wrong, either. Percentageally speaking, that's, like, a perfect score."

Kiki rolled her eyes, then addressed Mr. Mazer. "But how can we have a winner if we haven't even had a contest yet?"

"No, no, Mr. Piddles is correct," Mr. Mazer replied. "You ladies haven't learned a thing."

"With all due respect, sir, I'm not sure that's true," I countered. "At least our team's learned a lot." I turned to Beanpole in order to prove a point. "What's the primary chemical compound used in table salt?"

"May I have a definition, please?"

Note to self: smash Beanpole in the shins later.

"Congratulations, Lady Aardvarks. I know you'll represent our school well."

We glanced around at one another with bewildered looks.

"Grover Park Middle School will be sending just one team to compete this year, and that team is..." Mr. Mazer paused for dramatic effect.

Kiki scowled at me. "Prepare to polish, nerdvark."

"Eat mud, snoot queen."

"All of you."

"Excuse me?" Brattany said.

Yeah, what'd he mean by that? I thought.

"That's right," Mr. Mazer explained. "You are all winners today. The six of you are going to form one unified team."

"What?!" Kiki said.

"Isn't that exciting?" Mr. Mazer replied with an ear-to-ear smile.

"No," Kiki replied.

"See, three students isn't enough, anyway, but six—now that's a team." We looked at one another, shocked and horrified. "But do you really want to know why we've decided to go this route, ladies? Do you really want to know?"

I looked at Mr. Piddles, and like magic, the answer came to me.

"Because it's just," I replied.

"That's right, Miss Saunders. Because you deserve one another," Mr. Mazer said. "You girls deserve one another more than soup deserves a spoon. More than cereal deserves milk. More than rhinoceroses deserve those tiny little birds that pick the unchewed food out of their teeth."

"That's gross," Beanpole said.

"Rhinoceros horn is good for your estrogen levels," Q replied.

"Yep, you were born to be teammates," Mr. Mazer informed us.

"But . . . But . . ."

"No buts," he interjected. "My decision is final. From this moment forward, the six of you will be our Academic Aardvarks." Mr. Mazer flexed his muscles and roared. "Aardvark power . . . *Raaahhhh!*"

"Forget it. We'll polish," Kiki said.

"Sorry, Miss Masters, that deal is off the table. Seems someone has a father who's a lawyer, and he threatened to sue this school all the way to Singapore if his daughter touched even one bottle of glass cleaner," Mr. Mazer said, gazing at Brattany.

She slinked down in her chair.

"So, you're all winners today," he continued. "It's the Academic Septathlon or else."

"Fine, I'll take the *or else*," Kiki said disrespectfully. She turned to Brattany. "I mean, if he can't make us polish, then—"

"—Then you are going to be suspended from school for two weeks with an inquiry into expulsion from the district," Mr. Mazer answered, completing her sentence in a voice that was one hundred percent serious.

Kiki whipped her head around. "What? Why? You can't do that!"

"Destroying campus property. Trespassing in the art room. Incurring expensive overtime costs for noncertified personnel. Should I go on?" he asked. "If you'd like, I can have my secretary type up a list of potentially criminal infractions."

None of us replied.

"Ah, the sound of student silence. It's so rare on this campus. Makes me think we're all done here. Mr. Piddles, anything you'd like to add?"

"Feels just to me," he responded.

Is that the Declaration of Independence on his tie?

"And you, Mr. Stone. Anything you'd like to add before I send these ladies on their way?"

"My last stupid year," Mr. Stone mumbled.

"You'll find that your new Academic Septathlon coach is quite the inspirational leader," Mr. Mazer said.

Our coach?

"I mean, any man who draws a school paycheck should do the job he's assigned, to its utmost, wouldn't you say, ladies?"

Mr. Stone shifted in his seat and groused some more. Clearly, our principal and our vice principal had some stuff going on between them that we were getting caught in the middle of.

"May the wind be at your backs, Lady Aardvarks. I look forward to seeing your performance. And, oh yeah," he added, "if you don't finish in at least fourth place, we're going to revisit the idea of stern consequences."

Fourth place? Why?

"There will be no 'phoning it in,'" Mr. Mazer explained. "You will genuinely try to excel or you will genuinely pay the price."

The six of us exited the principal's office in a stupor, not quite sure what to say. Awkward silence filled the air.

Until it was broken by perk.

"I think it's a great idea!"

"No, it's not, Beanpole," I said. "It's the worst idea ever. I'd rather polish."

"So not fair," Q said. "We were gonna cream them, anyway."

"Were not," Kiki said.

"Were too," I told her.

"Were not," Brattany insisted.

"Stop!" Beanpole shouted. "Am I the only one who is sick of all this fighting?"

"I am," Sofes said meekly. Everyone turned to look at her. "Sick of all the fighting, I mean," she added sheepishly.

Kiki threw Sofes a glare filled with daggers.

"We can be a team," Beanpole argued. "We'll be unified. We'll be, like, the six Aardvark-e-teers, one for all and all for one."

She started to chant our school cheer.

"We're the Aardvarks,
   The mighty, mighty, Aardvarks!
   We're the Aardvarks,
   The mighty, mighty, Aardvarks!"

"How 'bout it?" Beanpole asked, a serving of extra perk on top.

We paused and slowly looked at one another. Kiki was the first to speak.

"Suck lemons, Beanpole. Skinny-chubby's right. This is a disaster." Kiki turned to her two pet ding-a-lings. "Come on, girls, we are outee."

And with that, the ThreePees marched off.

On Saturday, we sat at a rectangular brown table near the back of the library, waiting to have our first study session with the Wicked Witches of the West.

They were late. Of course.

"So, you gonna text him back?" Beanpole asked as I looked at my phone.

"Dee-leet," I replied, pushing a button.

"Mo, isn't this whole dee-leet thing with your dad getting a little old?" she asked.

"Not to me," I said. "But if he stops sending me messages, I promise I'll stop deleting them."

"Ssshh . . . here they come," Q said, interrupting us. "Quick, look intimidating."

"Intimidating?"

"Yeah, make them fear the nerd herd." Q lowered her chin,

squinted, and flashed her best *Don't mess with me* face. I watched as she contorted her body into all kinds of angles.

"Downright menacing," I said. "I'll be surprised if they even have the nerve to sit down."

She reached for her scuba tank. *Wheeesh-whooosh. Wheeesh-whooosh.*

"Oh yeah. That helps, too."

Kiki, leading the way, bounded into a chair and tossed down her backpack. Brattany and Sofes, flanking her, took seats as well—one on Kiki's left, one on Kiki's right—and tossed down their backpacks, too. It was three of us on one side of the table and three of them on the other, with about three feet of desktop space in the middle separating us.

"First rule: no phones," Kiki said, looking at Beanpole firmly gripping her cellie.

"Number one," I answered. "You don't make the rules. And number two, you're late."

"What are you talking about? It's quarter after two, just like we said," Brattany responded.

Q raised her wrist and read the digits on her calculator watch. "The current time is 2:17 and 36, 37, 38"—*Wheeesh-whooosh. Wheeesh-whooosh*—"41, 42, 43 seconds."

Kiki stared at Q with a puzzled, semimortified look. Beanpole, always the peacemaker, tried to explain nicely.

"Accurate statistics are important to her."

"Is any of that," Brattany said, pointing at Q, "contagious? 'Cause, like, if I catch something, my dad's a lawyer."

"I'd rather have her on my team than you," I shot back.

"And I'd rather not have any of you on my team," Kiki said.

"So we agree there. But our principal, Mr. Moron, has us backed into a corner, so let's just get to it so we can get it over with, okay?" She flipped though her nine-thousand-page binder. "I've already decided that the best way to do this, since we only have about three weeks, is to just split it up. We'll study Art, Theater, and Music; you take Science, Math, Language Arts, and History."

"No way," I replied. "Why should you get all the easy subjects while we do the hard ones?"

"She didn't say *moo-sic*, skinny-chubby. Like, of course, if food was a category, we'd let you take it," Brattany said to me.

Kiki laughed. "Double-double nice-nice," she said as she and Brattany high-fived.

"Come on, you guys," Beanpole pleaded. "We need to be a team."

"That's right," Sofes said. "Just like there's no shimmer in your hair if there's no *H* without the *p*."

The entire table stopped.

"Huh?"

"You know, healthy hair? It's pH-balanced," Sofes explained. "You can't just have the *H*." She flipped her notebook open to a blank page. "Like, duh," she added, as if her point were so obvious.

"Sofes, do you know about anything other than hair?" Kiki inquired in a condescending tone.

"Hmm . . . let's see." Sofes looked up. "Do the physics of jet propulsion count?"

"You know about the physics of jet propulsion?" Beanpole asked, impressed.

"No, I was just wondering if that would have counted." Sofes and Beanpole paused, looked at one another, and then, at the same exact time, smiled.

"*Hee-hee,* I'd give you credit," Beanpole said.

"Wow, propulsion," Sofes replied. "I can't believe I knew such a sophisticationed word."

The two of them giggled some more as Brattany glanced at Kiki with an *I knew this was going to happen* look on her face.

"You know, there ought to be a rule that punishes your parents for the damage they're causing to society," Kiki said to Sofes.

Rule? Q pricked up her ears, and I could see the little hamster wheel spinning in her head.

"Academic Septathlon bylaws state that each team must operate in a system whereby the distribution of"—*Wheeesh-whooosh. Wheeeh-whooosh*—"questions is evenly split between all contestants, meaning an order must be established, and that order cannot be altered or deviate at any juncture of the competition."

"Like, what is wrong with the allergy freak?" Brattany asked.

"Yeah, do we need to put her in a plastic bag or something?" Kiki wondered. "Of course, we'd poke holes in it so she could breathe."

"Tiny ones," Brattany added with a smile.

"She's talking about the rules, snobwads," I said. "We have to go in a specific, predetermined order; otherwise we forfeit."

"But there's six of us," Sofes said.

We all paused.

"So?"

"So, doesn't that mean we'd have to six-feit? You know, not four-feit but six-feit? *Tee-hee.*"

"Okay, she goes last," I said.

"Hallelujah, the first thing we agree upon," Kiki said, throwing her hands in the air.

Beanpole locked eyes with me in one of those disapproving, motherly glares.

"What?" I said

"Don't be mean, Mo. Being mean is not nice."

"Being mean is not nice?" I said. "What are we in, second grade?"

However, Beanpole was entirely serious. "That is correct," she answered. "Being mean is not nice."

I let out a sigh. Deep down, I knew Beanpole was right. It was just that the ThreePees always seemed to bring out the worst in me. Why did I let those girls get under my skin the way they did?

"Finally, our coach," Kiki said, noticing that Mr. Stone had entered the library. "Maybe he can snap you dipsticks into shape."

"You're the dipsticks," I said.

"No, you are!"

"You are!"

"Hey, hey, hey!" Vice Principal Stone said, walking up to our table. "Now, let's get one thing straight. I may be the coach on paper, but let me tell you, I only have six months before retirement, and I have no plans to do squat with any of this contest nonsense."

"Huh?" We stared. Having a coach was a big part of the Academic Septathlon.

"That means, don't ask me questions, don't bring me problems, and don't get me involved in any aspect of this," he instructed. "You are absolutely and entirely on your own."

Mr. Stone scanned the library to make sure the conversation wasn't being overheard.

"And if you tell anyone, I'll make sure every official document that says you ever attended this school vanishes from the system," he threatened. "You'll be like ghosts. No transcripts, no records, not even a photocopy of your birth certificate will exist, you understand me?"

We stared, wide-eyed.

"Oh, believe me, I can do it," he said confidently. "You'd be amazed at the power of cyberspace to suck data into places where it will never be seen again." Mr. Stone adjusted the knot of his tie and straightened it. "The last thing I want right now is to be some lame coach in some lame trivia game for a bunch of mean-spirited, wannabe Einsteins, got it?"

"Yes, sir," we softly replied.

"Good. You'll only see me twice. Once now and once on the night of the competition, where we're all going to pretend that we've worked really hard putting in lots of long hours, like good little goofballs. Otherwise, *zap!* Your files will disappear into the black hole of the Internet."

Mr. Stone buttoned his coat and checked his wristwatch. "By the way, why are you still even here?" he asked.

"Um," I said, "we're studying?"

"But you've got to get over to the Civic Center to register by six tonight, or you won't be eligible."

"We do?" None of us had heard about this.

"Ah jeez, this is exactly what I mean," he said, throwing up his hands. "If you don't hightail it over to the Civic Center to register within the next eighty-seven minutes, you won't be allowed to participate. Holy cow, don't you know that the Academic Septathlon is governed by rules, rules, rules?"

"But, like, don't *you* need to be there to sign some documents or something for us?" Brattany asked.

"Have Kiki forge them," he replied. "I mean, she forges her parents' signatures all the time, anyway. How hard can mine be?"

Kiki sheepishly looked down as Mr. Stone grumbled something I couldn't quite make out and then walked off.

Great, I thought. We were now coachless.

The other girls started calling their parents right away, to see which of them could drop everything and drive us over to the Civic Center. I didn't dare call my house.

"And why is that?" Beanpole asked, her hands on her hips.

"Because dear old Dad might show up wanting to fill a hole or something," I replied honestly.

She shook her head. "I bet if he knew you just said that, he'd be hurt."

"And I bet if I even knew him AT ALL, I'd care."

I popped a piece of saltwater taffy into my mouth. I'd always liked saltwater taffy. Number one, it's taffy. Yum. Number two, it is practically a zero-fat food item. Of course, it is also a zero-nutrition food item, but considering that it must have come from the ocean—I mean, why else would they call it saltwater taffy (like, duh)?—how unhealthy could it really be?

Okay, maybe Beanpole had a point, but I hadn't really come

to terms with how I felt about my father. However, he'd been gone for years and years, so I should at least have had that much time to figure it all out on my end, no?

Or at least months and months.

Weeks and weeks?

"Mo, please don't take this the wrong way," Beanpole said in a kind, sympathetic, might-become-a-kindergarten-teacher-one-day type of voice, "but you have issues."

"Beanpole, you alphabetize your underwear, so when it comes to having issues, let's just agree that I'm not alone, all right?"

Q hung up her phone. "My mom's on her way. She'll be here in ten."

"You see?" I said. "Problem solved. Let's go wait by the carpool loop." The three of us grabbed our backpacks and got ready to go.

"Shouldn't we, you know, offer them a ride?" Beanpole asked, sort of nudging over toward the ThreePees.

"Let them hitchhike," I said. "With any luck, some campfire-story guy with one eye and a rusty chainsaw will pick them up."

Q smiled. When it came to the way we felt about the Three-Pees, she and I were *simpático*. (That's Spanish for "on the same page.")

"Come on, you guys, they're our teammates. And like it or not, we're going to have to start working with them." Beanpole turned toward the ThreePees and cheerily called out, "Hey, you need a ride?"

Sofes twirled around and smiled. "Um, yeah, I think we actually—"

"Eat a molded muffin, Beanpole," Kiki said as she stepped in front of Sofes. "My sister will be here in five." She put her phone into her back pocket and stared at Sofes with a *What are you doing?* look on her face. Sofes hung her head and shrugged.

"See?" I said to Beanpole as I headed through the silver turnstile, "you can't be nice to them. It doesn't pay."

Before we knew it, Q's mom, Mrs. Applebee, picked us up in what we had affectionately named the Nerd Mobile. Really, the car was nothing more than a four-door blue import with leather seats and cup holders for every passenger, but once we'd given the car this nickname a couple of months earlier, the joke had sort of stuck.

We climbed in and put on our seat belts.

"Are you okay, Alice? You know I'll always drop everything to come and get you right away. You know that, right?"

"I'm fine, Mom," Q replied. "We just needed a ride."

"Are you sure you're feeling okay?" Q's mother asked. "I noticed you wheezing last night."

"I'm fine, Mom." Q rolled her eyes. "Fine. We're going to be late."

After a silent mother-daughter battle of wills, where Q's mom communicated through eye contact that she was highly concerned for Q's health, and Q responded by dismissing her mother's phobia, averting her gaze and looking out the window, Mrs. Applebee put the car in gear and we drove away.

By 5:35, we'd arrived at the Civic Center, a crisp white building that Grover Park had built a few years earlier in an attempt to attract some fancy theater productions to the area. Broadway revival shows like *Cats* and musicals that old people loved, like *Oklahoma!*, played there practically every other month. But there were minor shows that played there, too, like B-level circus shows where the elephants were blind, and international dance troupes featuring ballerinas from countries no one had ever heard of, like the Republic of Nauru.

Two years ago, for my birthday, my mom took me to see a production of *Peter Pan*, but the stage ropes weren't working that night, so the actors couldn't even fly. There's nothing more pathetic than a nonflying Peter Pan. Captain Hook should have kicked his scrawny butt. Plus, Tinker Bell should have suffered a beat-down, too. I mean, what kind of wimp can't stomp a nonflying fairy?

Carnegie Hall this theater was not.

Kiki and her coconuts beat us to the Civic Center, so by the time we arrived and walked inside the main lobby, they had already been to the registration table and picked up all the forms. The place was buzzing with activity. Nine different middle schools would be competing in the California Region Eight showdown, and you could feel the energy and excitement in the air. Parents swirled about; coaches addressed their teams, giving them instructions and pep talks. We were the only group of kids that was just a group of kids, with no adults to guide our way. Mrs. Applebee had decided to run to the drugstore to get eucalyptus drops to put into Q's air purifier as a way to help her with the wheezing, and said she'd pick us up in forty-five minutes, despite the fact that Q said she didn't want any eucalyptus drops and wouldn't use them. So we huddled off to the side and tried to figure everything out by ourselves.

Kiki passed out two forms to each of us that needed to be signed and returned by the following Wednesday.

"The first's a registration and grade-verification form," she explained, "and the second is a parent permission slip to appear on TV."

"We're going to be on TV?" Q asked, her eyes big.

"Calm down, goober," Kiki answered. "It's only a local community station, like channel 723 or something."

"Yeah," Brattany said. "Only about thirty-eight people ever watch it, and most of them are old folks in nursing homes who drool."

Q turned to me for support. I knew how much she dreaded appearing in front of crowds. *Wheeesh-whooosh. Wheeesh-whooosh.* "TV?"

"It'll be fine," I told her, with a false confidence. "Don't worry."

But of course, I was worried, too. Appearing on TV could mean only one thing: I needed to lose some weight.

And fast.

I immediately made a plan to eat only celery stalks for the next thirteen days, supplemented with small sips of water. Then on day fourteen, I'd give up the celery and go with just straight H_2O until the competition. Perhaps I could even cut the $_2$ in the H_2O and just go with HO. I bet that would help trim flab faster. I knew I'd need all the help I could get, because I'd heard that TV cameras put ten pounds on you.

Ten pounds? How unfair is that? I mean, if something is going to add ten pounds to my body, shouldn't I at least get the pleasure of its being soaked in caramel and traveling over my taste buds?

"Oh, look. If it isn't Kiki Masters."

"Well, if it isn't Wynston Haimes," Kiki responded.

A dark-haired girl with sparkling green eyes approached. She was wearing a navy blue schoolgirl uniform accented by a crisp white shirt with tasteful red trim on the collar. On her chest was an embroidered *SD*, the initials of her school, and on her feet were a pair of chocolate-brown penny loafers that must have cost $350.

Of course, the kicker was the knee-highs.

It takes a lot of guts to wear knee-high socks when you're our age—a lot of self-confidence, too—and not every girl has the legs to make them look good.

Wynston made them look great. I could tell right away by the manner in which she approached, with her army of knee-high-wearing junior bunny rabbits following closely behind, that we were looking at the ringleader of the Saint Dianne's team.

"Competing in the Septathlon, are you, Keeks?" Wynston's classmates formed a wall of crisply dressed private-school prigs behind her. And yes, it was intimidating.

"Competing? No," Kiki answered. "Winning? Yes."

Wynston and her henchgirls laughed.

"Oh, you've got to love that public-school spunk, don't you?" Wynston said. "Well, losing won't sting too bad, Kiki. I mean, you've got to be getting used to it by now."

Ouch. The girls from Saint Dianne's snickered. Kiki and Wynston had a history that went back to cheerleading camp, where they had gone toe to toe for the past two summers to see who would be named head cheerleader of the city's formidable intramural squad.

Both times, for division six and division seven, Wynston Haimes had eked out a close victory over Kiki.

"Well, here's a little FYI and four-one-one you can take to the B-A-N-K," Beanpole suddenly blurted out, as she stepped forward and crossed her arms in a *Take that!* manner. "The Aardvarks are on a mission to make some whomp-'em powder!"

Beanpole turned to high-five Q. They raised their hands for a *That's what I'm talkin' about, baby* hand slap.

But missed. Beanpole nearly fell into a table.

"Don't worry, don't worry, I'm okay," she said, regaining her balance. Then, remembering how to deal with such situations, she slowly spread her arms, stood on one foot, and began to chant, "*Ommmmmm.*"

Wynston lowered her chin and looked us over, first Beanpole, then me, then Q.

In response to the scrutiny, Q took a scuba dive. *Wheeesh-whooosh. Wheeesh-whooosh.*

"New chums, Keeks?"

"Not hardly," Kiki answered, as if we were nothing but pieces of garbage.

"Well, I do hope that you and your band of tragics aren't too embarrassed come competition night," Wynston replied. "I mean, it must get so tiring being defeated by me all the time."

Wynston smiled. Her teeth were beautiful, like fine jewelry.

"Times change," Kiki answered defiantly.

Wynston took a second gaze at me and my nerd herd.

"Indeed they do, Keeks. Indeed they do."

"Come, come girls," the coach of Saint Dianne's said to her team, with a clap of her hands, as she walked up with the requisite registration forms. "I've scheduled a nutrition break of artisanal salads in twenty minutes, and then we'll do a study session on Greek rhetoric."

Beanpole leaned in to ask me a question, trying to speak in a low voice so no on else could hear. "What's *rhetoric*?"

"Yeah," Sofes said, overhearing. "And what language is Greek?"

Wynston smiled again. "Ciao, Keeks." With her army of identical soldiers following immediately behind, she began to walk away.

"Eat lint, Wynston!" Kiki cried.

Wynston stopped, turned, and grinned.

"So cultured, they are," she said to her navy blue crew. "Must be a class they insist upon campuswide."

The girls from Saint Dianne's swished away, swirling their skirts from side to side with every step.

"Note the purses," Kiki said to Brattany as she crossed her arms.

"François Fumeil?" Brattany replied.

"Yep. Straight from Paris," Kiki replied. "I want one, like, so bad."

"How much?" Brattany asked.

"Six hund-ee," Kiki replied. "If you can even find one."

Kiki and Brattany continued to stare at the girls from Saint Dianne's. Their envy oozed.

"Sheesh, they're even more stuck up than you," I said. "I didn't think that was possible."

"Put a sock in it, Maureen."

"And, like, way to stick up for your teammates, too," I added. "Real cool the way you hung us out to dry."

Kiki spun around and jumped in my face. "Look, we're not teammates, we're not friends; we're nothing other than a bunch of kids thrown together who are trying to avoid being suspended from school; you got it, skinny-chubby?"

"You should think about seeing the school counselor, you know that, Kiki?" I said. "I mean, you realize they've been specially trained to deal with psychopaths like yourself, right?"

Kiki sniffed and grabbed her backpack. "Just make sure you and your band of gecknods know the material," she ordered. "It's embarrassing enough having to appear with nerds, but having to appear with nerds who aren't even supergeniuses, well, that just takes the Christmas cake." She turned to her donkeys. "Come on, ladies. We are outee."

And without a good-bye or a "see ya tomorrow," the Three-Pees were gone.

"But we are, too, smart," Beanpole said. "I mean, I have a 3.92 GPA."

"Four point"—*Wheeesh-whooosh. Wheeesh-whooosh.* "Oh."

"You have a perfect 4.0?" I said to Q. "Like, you've never even had a B plus?"

"Nope. Never will, either." Q reached into her backpack and pulled out a cylindrical container filled with a weird-looking brown liquid. "Education was important to my dad. I'd die before I'd get less than an A now."

She withdrew a straw. Not just a regular old straw, though. Always having to be different, she pulled out one of those twisty, swirly straws that make whatever you're drinking look like it's on a crazy roller-coaster ride before it hits your mouth.

"And that is...?" I asked, watching a swoosh of brownish liquid travel up and around and sideways before entering her mouth.

"Almond milk?"

"Allergy fighting?" I asked.

"Double bonus of being brain juice, too," she answered. "I think Barbara's right. It's time to break out the whomp-'em powder."

A smile came to Beanpole's face, and she started excitedly clapping her hands like a five-year-old who had just found out the whole family was going to go out for ice cream. She and I knew that Q was the smartest of all of us, and that she was going to set her mind to actually kicking some butt at the Academic Septathlon.

"Your doctors give you that?" I asked, staring at the sludgy-looking mush she was consuming.

"Cashews," she answered.

"Excuse me?"

"It's got ground-up cashew nuts in it," she said. "You see how my mom is getting more and more obsessive? Time for me to step up the plan."

I knew Q was just avoiding my question about her doctors, but her message was loud and clear: whatever she was doing in her quest to help her mom, she was going to do it whether I thought she should or not.

"Beanpole," I said. "Get your phone."

"Got it," she said, whipping out her cellie. "Why, Mo?"

"Just make sure you've got 9-1-1 on speed dial," I told her, gazing at Q. "For more immediate medical attention, that is."

Q reached into her backpack, took out a bag of peanuts, and popped one into her mouth, just to show me what she thought of my commentary. She washed it down with her new brown-sludge drink. "Cheers," she said.

Once again, I found myself watching the liquid travel up, down, and around the roller coaster before hitting her mouth.

"Come on, let's go, guys," Beanpole said. "Your mom's gonna be here any minute, Alice."

With only a few weeks to go before the competition, we exited the Civic Center. I was entirely confident that we held a supreme and unchallenged hold.

On ninth place.

he next day at 2:15, the six of us gathered in the public library, since the school was closed. Teacher workday.

"So, when we tackle the history section," Kiki began, "I'll go first, then Brit, then—"

"Wait a minute," I said. "Who put you in charge?"

"Look, the rules say we need a captain in case any important decisions come up," Kiki answered. "And clearly, I'm the most fit."

"You mean you're the most self-absorbed," I replied.

"She's not my captain," Q said. "Maureen should be our leader."

"Me?"

Q nodded and took a swirly sip of magic nut juice.

"No way," Brattany answered. "I'm not following anyone who wears plus-size jeans. My father says it shows weak character."

Ouch. I'm not sure if people who don't struggle with their weight understand how much comments like that hurt.

"And he should know, 'cause he's a lawyer," Brattany added. Just. So. Mean.

"You ever think that maybe it's people who judge other people by the size of their jeans who have the weak character?" Q asked, coming to my defense. She must have seen the sting of Brattany's words on my face.

Brattany considered it. "Nope. Fat kids are pretty much lame. And by the way, what's in that thing, anyway?" she asked, pointing at Q's scuba tank. "Alien particles that allow you to breathe our air?"

"Stop it," Beanpole said. "We've got to put aside our differences and become a team. The universe is all about oneness." She rose to her feet to give a General Patton–like victory cry. "Now, are we Aardvarks or not?"

Q and I crossed our arms and scowled. Why was Beanpole so thick about this stuff? Didn't she know oil and water did not mix?

"I said, are we Aardvarks or not? Come on, chant it with me.

> *"We're the Aardvarks,*
> *The mighty, mighty Aardvarks!*
> *We're the Aardvarks,*
> *The mighty, mighty Aardvarks!"*

At the end of the cheer, to really drive her point home, Beanpole leaped high in the air and cheered a big *YAY!*

But she smashed her knee into the table on the way up.

"Ouch!" she yelped. That one sounded like it hit marrow. "Don't worry, don't worry, I'm okay."

"Do you know how stupid that sounds?" Kiki said as she watched Beanpole hop up and down on one foot. "I mean, who on this green earth would actually want to be an Aardvark?" She popped an Oreo into her mouth. Every time we met, she'd eat a sleeve of those things, but the girl never put on an ounce of weight. What I wouldn't have given for her metabolism.

"I'm an Aardvark," Sofes said.

"What?" Kiki said, in the midst of another Oreo.

"I'm an Aardvark," Sofes repeated. "And you are too, Keeks. When you really think about it, we're all Aardvarks."

Beanpole, rubbing her knee, smiled.

Kiki contemplated the idea for a moment; then, after finishing her cookie, she took a tube of lip gloss out of her purse. Slowly, she applied a fresh coat of shine.

"Indeed, that might be true, Sofes. But let me tell you something about being an Aardvark," she said in an *I know something that you don't know* way. "I'm not brainless enough to like it."

"Yeah," Brattany confirmed. "Neither am I."

Sofes, quiet, hung her head.

"I need to pee," I said, rising to my feet, disgusted by pretty much everything I was seeing.

"But you just went," Kiki replied. "And we've got work to do."

"I'm hydrating," I said, pointing to my liter-size water bottle. Now that I knew I was going to be on TV, the idea of shrinking my tonnage consumed me, and drinking gallons of water was always rule number one for any diet. After all, the last thing I wanted was to look like a mama sea otter for my very first time on television.

"Hydrating?" Brattany said. "Looks more like you're bloating to me."

"Yeah, whatever you're doing, I think it's backfiring," Kiki added with a laugh.

"Actually, I don't need to pee, Kiki," I said matter-of-factly. "I just really need to get away from you for a few minutes."

"The feeling's mutual, skinny-chubby," Kiki replied. "Take your time."

Oh, how I wished she and I could switch body shapes for the rest of the year. Wouldn't that teach her a lesson?

"I'm coming with you," Q said, standing up.

Beanpole, unsure of what to do, took a moment to consider whether or not she should stay at the table or join us.

After a moment of, I assume, debating oneness with the universe, Beanpole sighed and rose from her chair. Clearly, she wished things were going more hunky-dory between all of us. But clear, too, was the sense that a homicide might occur at any moment. Slowly, and without saying a word, Beanpole walked with us to the bathroom. For the first time in my life, I kept my sarcastic comments to myself. This whole thing was getting way too intense for humor.

My phone buzzed. I looked at the screen.

"Figures," I said, when I saw it was my father calling. "I mean, who in the world would have ever thought that speaking to him might actually be a more pleasant conversation than the one I was just having?"

"You're going to answer?" Beanpole asked. I looked at Kiki across the library. She glared.

"Of course not," I said. "I mean, it's all his fault, anyway."

"What does that mean?" Beanpole asked, looking at me like I was nuts.

"Nothing," I said as I pushed the mute button. "Just drop it, okay? With my caloric intake this greatly diminished, I can't really be held responsible for what comes out of my mouth right now. It's hard enough to monitor what goes in."

Five seconds later, my phone buzzed again, notifying me that I had a new voice-mail message. I put my cellie back in my pocket, telling myself I'd delete it later.

After school let out the next day, being gluttons for punishment, my crew and I met with the wenches in the library again. We knew that we had no choice but to work together so that we could at least scratch our way into fourth place in three weeks. If this was Mr. Piddles's idea of justice, justice was a mighty cruel beast.

"Okay," Kiki said, taking the lead once again. "The subject is math."

"Did you say *math*?" I asked.

"Yes, I said math," Kiki replied, exasperated. "I am not saying I am the captain; I am simply saying we are going to study a key area of the test right now—unless, of course, you have a problem with that, Maureen?"

"Nope, no problem," I answered. "I just want to be ready."

Q, Beanpole, and I reached into our backpacks and took out our calculators. The ThreePees stared.

"Um, what are you doing?" Brattany asked.

Q took a sip from her swirly-strawed container of cashew-flavored almond mud, opened her binder, and began to read.

"'Competitors are permitted to use basic four-function calculators, provided that they supply their own, as they will not be'"—*Wheeesh-whooosh. Wheeesh-whooosh*—"'given on site to contestants who fail to bring one, and should a calculator fail, the student must'"—*Wheeesh-whooosh. Wheeesh-whooosh*—"'continue with the contest, as replacements are prohibited and will not be provided.'"

"Just getting our calculators," I said to the snoots across the table. "I mean, if we're allowed to use them, we should, right?"

Brattany, Kiki, and Sofes exchanged confused looks. Clearly, they hadn't known this rule.

And clearer still was the fact that they hadn't brought calculators to the study session.

"Well, well, well, it seems the Dorkasaurus Mafia actually knows something, now, doesn't it?" I said, gloating.

"Don't get carried away, Nerd Girl," Kiki responded. "Come test day, we'll be sure to have calculators."

"There's other stuff, too," Beanpole said perkily. "Other strategies and stuff you should know."

"Like what?" Brattany asked in a snippy but curious tone.

"Don't tell them," Q said. "Those witches already—" She began to cough. It took a moment for her to catch her breath and finish her sentence. "They already know everything. Let them"—*Cough-cough*—"suffer."

"No," Beanpole said. "We should tell them. We're a team."

Q and I rolled our eyes. We knew Beanpole was right, but

still, I didn't want to share anything with these snots, much less the key ins and outs of the rules we'd spent so much time learning.

Beanpole, however, saw this as an opportunity to have some real group-bonding time, and she leaped at the chance.

She told them about the no-penalty-for-guessing rule, so that no matter what, we should always take a stab at a question, because points would be subtracted only for rule violations and not incorrect answers. She also told them about using the process of elimination to find right answers, because each question offered more wrong answers than right ones, so that if you looked for what was wrong as opposed to what was right, you could up your chances of success that way. And she taught them about trusting your instincts.

"Because research has proven," she said with extra perk, "that a student's first guess is most often the correct guess."

Kiki and Brattany might have had sneers on their face as they listened, but they paid attention, because Beanpole was relaying all sorts of critical information that solid Septathlon contestants needed to know.

Essentially, Beanpole became an open book about sharing everything, and before the week was over, the six of us were actually studying together.

And improving.

Except for Sofes. She couldn't get an answer right if her life depended on it.

"The subject is science," Kiki began.

Sofes turned to Beanpole. "That's my worst one."

"You can do it, Sofes. You've been studying hard. Trust your instincts."

Kiki began to read:

"According to modern science, a change in allele frequencies in a population is called
a. evolution
b. directed selection
c. Neo-Darwinism
d. recombination
e. gene flow"

Sofes contemplated the question. "None of the above."

"That's not an option, Sofes." Kiki waited for a new response.

"Nope, I say that it's none of the above," Sofes replied, her confidence growing. "I don't think any of those answers are right, and my instincts tell me that they are using inverse psychiatry."

Kiki took a deep breath. "So, let me get this straight. In an *A/B/C/D/E* question, you are claiming that the correct answer is none of the above, like perhaps *F* is the answer choice?"

"Exactly," Sofes said. "I'm going off the board, and I'm gonna take answer choice *F*."

"I like her spirit," Beanpole said.

"You would," I replied.

"Sofes, I want you to go home, fall off your roof, and not heal until we can find a replacement," Kiki said to her.

"Really, we could bring a kangaroo to the Civic Center next week and I bet they'd get more answers right," Brattany added.

"So the answer's not 'none of the above'?" Sofes asked.

Brattany rubbed her temples as if this whole thing were giving her a migraine.

"Make sure the roof is at least four stories," Kiki said, pointing upward. "And lobby level doesn't count."

Sofes turned to Beanpole. "But it seemed like a trick question."

"Don't worry," Beanpole replied. "Lots of them do."

If Sofes was bad, Q was the exact opposite. It was like she had turned into a virtual answering machine. Ever since she'd shifted from learning the rules to learning the actual material, she was knocking out answer after answer.

"Wow," I said, after she aced a particularly challenging question on the Middle Ages.

"Yeah," she said, with a smile. "I guess I've just kind of got a knack for this."

"Well, they do say that alien life is supposed to be intelligent," Kiki sniffed.

"Whatever," I said. Of course, I knew that Q had been really cranking on the studying, because feeling prepared was her way of dealing with the stress of appearing on television. Every moment she intensely studied was one less moment she would spend worrying about stage fright. Brainiacism had become her antidote for nerves.

Well, that and a gallon of sludge every day. I swear she was gulping down that mystery mud like a fiend.

"Time for a break," I said, rising from my chair. "I need to—"

"We know, we know," Kiki said, filling in the rest of my sentence for me. "You need to pee."

"It's called biology, Kiki," I said, and then I whipped my head around to hit Beanpole with a pop quiz in order to keep her sharp. "Quick, name a species of bird where the male, the father, is the caretaker of the eggs."

"Your father."

"I just said it's the father, Beanpole. But name the species of bird."

"No, your father, Mo." She pointed toward the front. "He just walked into the library."

I turned. "OMG."

"That's your dad?" Kiki said. "I would have thought he'd be heavier."

I rolled my eyes but didn't have time to launch a verbal missile in Kiki's direction, because once my father located me, he started walking over, and I knew I had to intercept him right away. I mean, the last thing I wanted was for him to actually meet anyone.

"Excuse me," I said, rushing up to him. "Like, what are you doing here?"

"Well . . ." he said as I pulled him toward the nonfiction section, "can I just say that it sort of feels like you're avoiding me?"

"And can I just say that it feels like you keep popping up out of nowhere?" I backed up so that we were between the stacks. "Like, literally Out. Of. Nowhere." I made no attempt to hide my irritation.

"Um, okay . . . communication," he replied. "This is good."

I didn't respond. We stood there for a long, tense moment.

"Um, okay . . . no communication," he said. "Not so good."

I poked my head around the bookshelves and glanced over at

the Septathlon team, feeling embarrassed. After all, what could be more hideous than your long-lost, wanna-fill-some-holes father showing up at school just because he wanted to, like, get to know you?

So lame.

Kiki and Brattany tapped their wrists as if they were wearing watches, to let me know I should hurry. Sofes ran her fingers through her hair, checking the strands for split ends. Q and Beanpole, however, gazed at me with concern written all over their faces.

"Why are you here?" I asked, turning around to face my father.

"I wanted to see your school," he answered. "I've never been here before. It's, uh...nice."

He surveyed the library. I noticed he was wearing one of those stupid school name tags on his green shirt. The front office secretary must have made him stick it on after he showed some ID. His badge said, GROVER PARK MIDDLE SCHOOL VISITOR: MICHAEL ANDREW SAUNDERS.

That's when I realized that his initials were M.A.S. My initials are M.A.S., too, my middle name being Alexandra. I wasn't sure if I'd ever known that before.

"I gotta go," I said, shaking my head. *We shared the same initials?* This was just way too much.

"Wait," he replied, grabbing my arm. I lowered my eyes to the spot where his hand held on to me. He let go. "Can I ask you a question?"

"What?"

"Do we, you know . . . have a chance?"

Why did he have to do this now? I stared at my shoes, avoiding eye contact. It was a long time before I answered.

"I dunno."

He waited for more. There was no more, that was it.

"But that's not a no, is it?" he asked hopefully.

"It's not a yes, either," I said as I began to walk away.

"Wait," he said, grabbing my arm again.

I sighed. "What?"

"Will you see me?"

He let go.

"Huh?"

"A specific time. A specific place. Can you make a definite commitment to that, like a date?"

A date? I felt my jaw clench. *What to do, what to do?*

I guess it was inevitable that it would one day come to this, even though I had really hoped it wouldn't. I had grown up with a mom, not a dad. I loved my mom. Of course. But did I hate my dad? Not really. I'd just never really thought about him all that much. I'd never thought much about the fact that our family didn't own a pet parakeet, either. I mean, when you don't really have something in your life, you don't really miss it; but when you get what you never had, are you supposed to be happy about it? Or sad that you are just now getting what you should have had all along?

This whole hole-filling thing of his confused me. And I didn't want to find out if it would eventually make any sense, either.

"Okay," I replied.

He smiled.

Well, what was I supposed to do? He's my father.

"When?" he asked.

"Three weeks after my twenty-fifth birthday, I have an opening for lunch. But just a sandwich, not like a full sit-down meal."

His smile grew. "You always were the funniest in the family, dimps."

Well, maybe I didn't want to be funny. Maybe I wanted to be alluring or talented or exotic or glamorous. Screw funny. But, of course, how would he even know that, considering he'd been out of my life for, oh, like practically all of it?

My shoulder muscles got tighter and tighter.

"Maybe there's a question you want to ask me?" he asked

A question?

"G'head," he said. "I can take it."

"Here? Now?"

I peeked back at the girls. The ThreePees *harrumphed*, getting more and more annoyed that I was wasting their time. Q and Beanpole, however, looked more and more concerned for me.

"Really, I can take it, dimps," he said. "You know, holes to fill."

For the record, I officially hated how he called me dimps. I mean, what kind of stupid nickname was that to give a person, anyway? And why did he feel he was even allowed to give me a nickname? Maybe he could have started with giving me something a bit more practical, like bike-riding lessons or help with my math homework or . . .

I stopped, my entire body rigid. The anger in me was growing, and I hated when I felt like that. Being angry angered me, if that makes any sense, and the only thing I knew was that I didn't want to think about or talk about or deal with any of this stuff anymore.

Especially with him. *Why did he even have to come back?*

"Okay, I have a question," I said, an obvious edge in my voice. "Are you going to hurt Mom?" I glared. "Again?" I added.

Whoa. I could tell he hadn't been expecting that one. He ran his fingers through his hair and took a moment before answering.

"I'm going to try not to," he said.

I waited for more. There was no more. That was it. A moment later, I shook my head and started walking back to the table.

"Hey," he called. "Where are you going?"

"Date's off." Hopefully he had brains enough to figure out why. Trying not to hurt Mom wasn't good enough. He *had* to not hurt Mom.

I walked over to the study table without looking back, but I could feel my father's eyes following me. After I sat down in my chair, I stole a small glance in his direction.

But he was gone.

I scanned the room. Nothing.

I looked toward the front entrance. A blur of his green shirt caught my eye as the door closed behind him.

Yep, he was gone. Maybe forever. Maybe not. What did I know?

"Can we please get back to what we were doing?" Kiki yipped, as if she had about a thousand different places she'd rather be.

Beanpole stared at me compassionately. "You okay?" she asked, rubbing my back.

"I need chocolate," I said. "Large amounts."

"Trust me," Kiki answered. "No, you don't."

We'd barely survived two weeks of intense studying with the ThreePees.

"I hate them. I seriously hate them," I said as we sat in Beanpole's bedroom on the Sunday before the Septathlon. "It's only twenty-four hours, but I don't know if I am going to make it. In fact, I don't even know how I made it this far."

"We should invite them over and pull out their toenails," Q said, sitting in the corner like a mouse.

"I already did," Beanpole answered.

"What?" I exclaimed.

Beanpole flipped through the mountaineering section of her closet, seeking out a lightweight polyurethane jacket suitable for modest precipitation. "I invited them over," she repeated, like it was no big deal.

"You invited them here?" I asked. "When?"

"Any minute."

"Excellent," Q said. "It's toenail time."

"Stop that, Alice," Beanpole said. "It's not nice to be not nice. We're a team, remember?"

I rolled my eyes. Uh-oh, here we go, I thought. Time for another cheer.

> "We're the Aardvarks,
>   The mighty, mighty Aardvarks!
>   We're the—"

"Enough. We get it, Beanpole," I said, cutting her off. "And they agreed to this?" Something smelled fishy.

"Well...not exactly," Beanpole answered. "But Sofes has a plan."

"Did you say *Sofes* has a plan?"

The doorbell rang.

"That's them."

"Can't wait," I said. "Maybe we'll celebrate with hemlock."

"Or at least make them drink it," Q added. "I bet you..." She stopped to cough. "I betya I could sneak some into their energy drinks."

She reached for her scuba tank to absorb some inhibitors. *Wheeesh-whooosh. Wheeesh-whooosh.*

"Be nice, you two," Beanpole said. "They're our guests, remember."

"That's what the people at the Last Supper said about one of their guests, too," I remarked.

Beanpole pretended not to hear and disappeared downstairs. Q lowered her inhaler but still coughed.

"You okay?" I asked as she struggled to catch her breath. She'd been carrying this barking camel in her throat for more than a week now.

"I'm fine," she replied, taking a swirly-straw sip of her thing-amajiggy juice to clear her windpipe.

"You don't look fine," I told her. "In fact, you look kind of haunted-housey."

"Just the rain," she said. "When the wetness mixes with the cold, I—" She coughed.

And coughed and coughed. She could barely catch her breath.

"Are you sure you're okay?" I asked. "Maybe I should call your mom so—"

"I'm fine!" she snapped. But clearly she was not fine. I grew more concerned.

"You know she'd want me to," I said. Ever since I had become tight with Q, I felt that I owed it to her mother to let her know when her daughter wasn't doing well. With all we'd been through already this past year, I just felt like it was kind of expected of me to look out for her.

But of course, Q's whole goal was to reduce her dependence on her mother, not increase it, and even the suggestion that I might get her mom on the phone caused her to shoot daggers in my direction.

"Just zip your"—*Wheeesh-whooosh. Wheeesh-whooosh...* Q struggled to take a slurp off her scuba tank—"lips," she finally said. I watched as she wrapped her scarf more tightly around her neck. "I'll be fine."

"I'm calling," I said. "You look like you're about to faint." I reached for my cellie.

"Don't!" she ordered. We heard the rustle of the girls coming up the stairs. "And don't say anything in front of the"—*Wheeesh-whooosh. Wheeesh-whooosh*—"witches, either."

I stared at her, phone in hand.

"Got"—*Cough-cough*—"me?"

Reluctantly, just as the footsteps were getting ever so close, I put my phone away. "Yeah, I got you, Miss Stubborn."

"Look who's talking, " Q replied.

Is there anything more frustrating than wanting to strangle your NFF? Beanpole entered first.

"Come in, come in, there's plenty of room for everybody," she said with a bounce. Clearly, having this many people over to her house was the thrill of a lifetime for Beanpole.

The ThreePees entered slowly, cautiously. Kiki and Brattany gazed around, uncertain looks on their faces as they took in the wholesome pictures of sunflowers and the fluffy mint green pillows that complemented the room. Sofes, however, sported a pleasant, warm smile.

Kiki caught sight of Q. "She gonna yak?"

"Yeah," Brattany said, turning her shoulder away as if she didn't want to breathe in the same air. "Freako looks ready to go all projectile on us."

"She's fine," I said, dismissing their concerns. Why I was standing up for her instead of getting her home, or even to a doctor, was beyond me. I mean, where was the line between being a friend and, well...being a friend? "All right, let's get to it, already," I said, changing the subject. The ThreePees had only been in the room for thirty seconds, and already I was looking forward to the moment that they would leave.

"Yes, let's," Brattany said, reaching into her purse. Beanpole closed the door as Brattany raised her cell phone camera.

Raised her cell phone camera? Was she preparing to film something?

"Okay..." Kiki said, looking at me, waiting.

"Okay what?" I said.

"Okay...forfeit," she said.

"Forfeit? What are you talking about?" I said. "We're not forfeiting."

"Of course you are," Brattany said from behind her camera. "Why else would we be here other than to hear you say you quit so we don't get into trouble with Mr. Moron?"

"I wouldn't quit if you"—*Wheeesh-whooosh. Wheeesh-whooosh*—"set my hair on fire," Q declared through a cough. "Give me some matches and I'd be glad to do the honor."

"You want a match, Brattany? My butt and your face," I said.

"Oh, yeah?" Kiki said. "Well, let me tell you something, skinny-chubby. I've had just about enough of..." Suddenly Kiki stopped talking and spun around to face Sofes. Her eyes blazed. "You said they were quitting," she said.

"*Welllll...*"

"Well what, Sofes?"

"Yeah, like why are we here?" Brattany asked, lowering her camera.

"For uniforms?" Sofes answered. "I thought we should, you know, wear uniforms for solidarnity."

"She means solidarity," Beanpole said. "You know, so we can be a team. I mean, did you see how great Saint Dianne's looked? We need to be able to match up with them on every front."

"You mean you knew about this?" Kiki said to Sofes.

Sofes averted her eyes and quietly nodded. She and Beanpole had conspired to try to bring the groups together. She had gotten Kiki and Brattany here by telling them the Nerds had decided to forfeit.

"Has the last brain cell in your mental boat finally abandoned ship? I mean, you know how I feel about—"

Suddenly, there was a voice from outside the door.

"Who's ready for a snacky-wacky?"

Department Store Mom, her timing perfect as usual, entered carrying a tray filled with homemade raspberry tarts. "They're scrumalumptious."

Kiki's jaw practically dropped when she saw Beanpole's mom. A red-checked apron. A matching red-checked hair band. A smile that looked as if she were ready to sell home appliances in a 1950s magazine. The expression on Kiki's face said it all: *You can't be serious.*

Oh no, I thought, shaking my head. Here we go.

"I made *treeeee*-eats," Department Store Mom said in a bubbly voice.

"Yay! Friendship tarts," Beanpole exclaimed, taking the tray of goodies from her mother.

"And I'll be back in a flash with the other stuff," Beanpole's mom said as she exited the room. "Jeepers, I'm practically tingling."

"Thanks, Mommy." Beanpole, smiling from ear to ear, began explaining the theme of today's treats as she held out the silver serving tray for all of us to see. "Six girls, twelve hands, all joined together and cherishing the oneness of Aardvarkness."

"The oneness of Aardvarkness?" Kiki asked.

No, I thought. No.

"Did you really just say 'oneness of Aardvarkness'?" Kiki inquired.

"Yep," Beanpole replied, with extra perk on top. "It's today's motif."

"Hey, Keeks..." Brattany said, picking up a tart.

"Hold on," Kiki responded as she stared in disbelief at Beanpole.

"No, Keeks, really," Brattany said. "You gotta see this."

"One sec, Brit," Kiki told her. "I'm still dealing with this whole 'oneness of Aardvarkness' thing."

"You mean theme," Beanpole said, correcting Kiki. "Putting themes in the food is a way of making sure all our efforts have a centralized pattern. I eat motifs all the time."

"Um, Kiki...I think this pastry is supposed to look like you."

"Huh?" Kiki turned and picked up a tart.

It did look like her. Matter of fact, for a baked-food item, it was a pretty good replica.

"You can't be serious," Kiki said, mortified by the pastry in her hand.

I lowered my eyes. See, in life, there are some swimming pools you have to enter from the shallow end, because jumping right away into the deep water might be overwhelming. That's how it was with Beanpole's house. Kiki needed to have started with something like a sip of iced oolong tea, or maybe taken a trip to the bathroom, where the toilet paper was folded into elegant, symmetrical triangles. But to dive right away into oneness-of-Aardvarkness-themed pastries that looked like her? Well, I could see why she was struggling.

"And they're made with one hundred percent organic ingredients, too," Beanpole added. "The berries are from our garden."

Kiki set down the tart. "Why are we here?" she said to Sofes.

"For the uniforms," Sofes answered. "You said yourself that at the talent show a few months ago the Nerd Girls looked pretty stylish. Barbara's mom made them."

"That doesn't mean I want to join the doofwad parade," Kiki snapped.

Brattany couldn't take her eyes off the tart that had been fashioned in her image. "She made a piece of food that looks like me. That's, like, creepy."

"I think it's nice," Sofes said. "I mean, your mom gives us snacks when we go to your house, Brit."

"Yeah, but she does what normal moms do; she buys them from the store. This is what stalkers who plan to eat their victims do," Brattany replied.

"Knockitty-knock." Department Store Mom reentered, carrying a box. "Oh, you girls are going to love what I have done with the uniforms. Trust me," she said, looking at Brattany. "You're going to look dee-licious."

Brattany edged backward, the look on her face saying it all: *Don't eat me.*

"Now, I guesstimated your blouse sizes based on your yearbook pictures, but I want to make sure that they fit properly, because first impressions always count." I could tell by the mile-wide grin on her face that Department Store Mom's perk-o-meter was cranked to full throttle. If ever I wondered where Beanpole had gotten her bubbles from, this was proof that they were woven into her DNA.

Kiki and Brattany hesitated, unsure of how to respond. However, Department Store Mom had plenty of experience in dealing with reluctant, snooty customers from back in the days when she worked in a retail store, so she handled the snobbery and standoffishness like a first-class pro.

"This will up your chances of winning a lot," Department Store Mom informed them. "Look good, feel good, project confidence, be confident, that sort of thing. Plus, you girls are so pretty," she said, speaking especially to Kiki and Brattany, "I'm sure you're just going to wow the entire television audience once you hit the stage."

Mentioning TV and appealing to their sense of vanity was smart. I could tell by the way the snobs were listening that the strategy was working.

"What do you say?" Beanpole's mom continued addressing Kiki specifically. "I mean, for a clothing designer, creating an outfit for someone with, how should I say this . . . with your athletic form . . . Well, I bet you could wear a tablecloth and make it look good."

Department Store Mom reached into a box and held up a long-sleeved black top that looked unlike any other piece of middle-school clothing I'd ever seen. Blazed across the front was our mascot, the Aardvark. Of course, normally, our mascot was the most pathetic creature ever invented. I mean, how many kids in this world are jealous of schools that have mules or earthworms for mascots? That's how bad it was for us at Grover Park. Our Aardvark was the saddest of the sad in a world filled with sad and bad.

But this Aardvark was growling.

And muscle-bound.

And had a look of fiery determination in its eyes. It was the most ferocious Aardvark I'd ever seen. Instantly, I loved it.

Two minutes later, Kiki was in the bathroom changing her clothes. When she walked out, I couldn't help saying, "Wow." I mean, if there had been a contest for best body in the school, Kiki would have won hands down.

"Talk about form-fitting," I said.

Kiki looked at herself in the full-length mirror, checking herself out from every angle.

"When you've got the form, it doesn't just fit, Nerd Girl," she said, making no attempt to hide how impressed she was with herself. "It *purrrrs*."

Brattany and Kiki smiled at one another. Their arrogance was unreal. But the outfit looked so good on Kiki, she decided to keep it on. Especially because any little help she could get to beat, or at least intimidate, Wynston Haimes and the snoots from Saint Dianne's was something she was going to seize.

"And now for these." Department Store Mom held up the pants she'd made to go with the top. They had a streak of fire running down the leg.

"Amazing, Mommy!" Beanpole said as she held the clothing up to her body.

"I didn't even think it was possible to make an Aardvark outfit look cool," I commented as Department Store Mom passed us our uniforms.

We took turns dashing into different rooms—the other bedrooms, the bathrooms—to get changed. The plan was that once we were in our uniforms we'd meet back in Beanpole's room so that Department Store Mom could inspect each of our outfits to figure out what slight adjustments were needed to get everything to look perfectly tailor-made.

Q disappeared into the master bathroom. When she came out, she looked transformed.

"Entirely nerdvarkian," she said through a cough.

"Fits great," I confirmed as I looked at myself in the mirror. This was a huge statement for me, because hating my body and hating the way I looked was pretty much how I always felt whenever I put on new clothes. After all, round is a tough shape to love. It was like there was a recording that always played in my head: *I would look so much better if only I lost a few more pounds.*

Literally, every time I looked in a mirror, the same tape played over and over.

I would look so much better if I lost a few pounds.

I would look so much better if I lost a few pounds.

I would BE so much of a better person if only I lost a few pounds.

The idea had been practically etched into my brain.

However, as Department Store Mom had taught me a couple of months back, dark tones slenderized, and the way she had put this whole outfit together, well . . . at least I didn't look like someone from Planet Fat Girl.

But still, I would have looked so much better if only I had lost a couple of pounds. (Like I said, permanent.)

Beanpole, having quickly changed, hustled back out. The clothes fit her like a glove.

"Hmm," Department Store Mom said. "I just got an idea about accessorizing. Back in a minute." She dashed off.

Her perk-o-meter screaming off the charts when she saw the six of us dressed in matching, awesome Aardvark uniforms, Beanpole started bobbing her head and began to chant.

"We're the Aardvarks,
The mighty, mighty Aardvarks!
We're the Aardvarks,
The mighty, mighty Aardvarks!"

"Don't get all nutso over there," Kiki said to Beanpole, still looking at herself in the mirror. "I'm only in it for the purse."

"The purse?"

"Yeah," Brattany replied. "Some old-timers' club is sponsoring a cash prize of $3,500 dollars to the winning team. Almost six hundred buck-a-roos to each of the contestants."

"They are?" I said.

"Turns out some geezers participated in Septathlon back in the nineteen hundreds or something and want to give back to education." Brattany checked out her butt in the mirror. Let's just say that Mother Nature had blessed her quite bountifully, too. "They're sponsors or something like that."

"Sponsors? More like suckers, if you ask me," Kiki said. "But if they are going to give me the cash to score a François Fumeil, I am gonna take the money and run." She smoothed out the sides of her pants. "I mean, why else do you think we're trying as hard as we are?

"I mean, come on," she continued, with a laugh. "You think we're in this for the school spirit?"

Kiki and Brattany giggled at the idea of it. However, just as they chuckled, they saw the smile fade from Beanpole's face.

"Oh, my gawd," Kiki said, shaking her head once she realized that school spirit was the exact reason Beanpole was so hypermotivated by this whole thing. "What a nerd."

"Yeah," Brattany chimed in. "Like Daddy always says, it's all about the cash, baybee."

Kiki and Brattany high-fived. "Double-double nice-nice," they said in unison.

Q's coughing spell began anew.

"Listen, you dorkwads, better show up big-time for the competition tomorrow," Kiki warned as she headed for the door. "And you better have your game faces on."

"Yeah," Brattany added. "If we are going to score some François Fumeil purses, your side of the ship has to step up."

"And that means we're counting on the alien," Kiki said, pointing at Q, "as well as praying for Einstein over here." She pointed to Sofes. "To hit a streak of luck."

Sofes looked down, embarrassed.

"Oh, I'll be there," Q fired back. "I'll be there in full—" *Cough-cough.* She couldn't even finish her thought.

"Don't strain yourself, weirdo," Kiki responded. "Come on, girls, we are outee."

"But what about the accessories?" Beanpole asked. "My mom will be back in a minute."

"You handle it," Kiki said. "For minor crud like this, Bean-pole, we trust ya."

"We'll let ourselves out," Brattany said, and a moment later, the three of them were gone.

Beanpole, Q, and I sat quietly in the room for a moment, staring at one another.

"Have I mentioned how much I hate them?"

As if having to deal with the ThreePees on a Sunday weren't bad enough, when I walked up to my house, the rain still drizzling, I noticed a silver BMW with black leather seats parked in the driveway.

Oh, great, time for more hole-filling.

I approached the front door. Why couldn't doughnuts be a diet food, I wondered as I put my key in the lock. I mean, really, we'd have so many more healthy people on this planet if they were.

I entered. Mom, Dad, and Ashley were sitting at the dining room table, looking through a bunch of flyers about gymnastics camps to send my sister to the following summer. Expensive, out-of-state stuff. I raised my hand before anyone could say a word.

"Hold on. Gotta pee."

I set my backpack down in its usual spot by the couch and headed for the bathroom. Come TV time tomorrow, I wouldn't be thin, but I certainly would have tried. It had been a bunch of days since I'd had a carb, a piece of chocolate, or a sugary soft drink, but after the show, someone would have to send a text message to every cupcake in town, letting them know that a maniac was on the loose.

I washed my hands, took a breath, and headed out to *face the fam*.

"Verdict," Ashley said as I approached the table. "Dad rocks." She moved aside some papers and showed me a brand-new tablet computer. "Wicked, huh? Top of the line."

"Where's Marty?"

"Spending the night at a friend's," Mom answered.

"Convenient."

"Don't start, Boo." A buzzer went off in the kitchen. "Hey, brownies are ready. Ashley, will you please come help me take them out?"

"Mom, you don't need me to help you take out the brownies. I want to show Maureen my new computer." Ashley turned to me. "And there's an app that gives me an allowance to buy other apps, so I can even load it up with—"

"Ash-leee," my mom said with an *I'm not fooling around here* tone in her voice. "I asked you to please come help me with the brownies. We need to cut them."

"But you don't cut brownies until they cool," Ashley replied, still not taking the hint.

"We'll fan them with place mats," Mom said. "One section of the pan at a time. Come."

I looked at my mother. "Subtle, Mom. Real subtle."

"I don't know what on earth you are talking about, Boo,"

she said, smoothing her blouse. "Ashley, put that down and go grab a spatula. Now."

A minute later, I was alone with my father, just as Mom had wanted. Was I even supposed to call him Dad? This was just weird.

"Nice computer, huh?" he said, to get some sort of conversation rolling.

"I guess," I replied. "I mean, I'm not the biggest tech dork ever."

"Nope, just a regular dork," Ashley said, popping her head in from the kitchen. "No need to leave this with you." She picked up her new tablet from the table. However, unable to resist temptation, she showed me the screen and started tapping away. "Check it out. There's also this new app where you can—"

"Ash-leee," Mom called from the kitchen.

"Coming, Ma-hmm," Ashley yelled. "I'll show you later," she said to me. She disappeared.

Once my sister was gone, there was an awkward silence.

"So, what kind of stuff do you like?"

Oh great, time for bonding. *Uncomfortable.*

"I dunno," I said, without much energy. All I really wanted was to eat an apple, take a bath, and get into bed. Tomorrow was a big day.

Of course, Dad kept pressing, though.

"You know, if you wanted a new computer, I could get you one, too," he offered.

"Marty says you're trying to buy our love."

"He said that?" my father asked, looking somewhat hurt.

"Is that what you're doing? Are you trying to buy our love?"

"You ask a lot of direct questions, don't you, dimps?"

Yup, he was trying to buy our love. I mean, if that was his answer, he definitely was trying to buy our love, right?

"No, I'm not trying to 'buy your love,' as Marty puts it." He ran his fingers through his hair. "I'm offering to buy you a computer. Not exactly the same thing." He played with his watchband for a moment, unbuckling the black leather strap, then refastening it. "Well, maybe I am trying to win you over a bit. Can you cut a guy some slack?"

I didn't answer.

"So, are you going to continue to avoid me?" he asked.

I want to.

Well, I didn't say that, but that's what I was thinking. I mean, it certainly seemed to be Marty's plan.

I had tried to talk to Marty about this whole situation. Three times. Once, he told me he was doing a project involving data structures for his AP science class and couldn't chat right then. The second time was the previous Saturday morning, when he told me we'd have to speak later, 'cause he was up until three a.m. and wanted to sleep in. The third time went something like this.

MARTY: Okay, I promise to meet you at Starbucks after school.

ME: You promise?

MARTY: I do. I really, really promise.

And then he didn't show up.

It stinks getting stood up by your own brother. It especially stank since he and I are kind of close. I mean, sure, he's tortured me my whole life, playing pranks and whatnot, but he's also been there for me and protected me. I thought this might be a time when I could maybe be there for him, like, return the favor. But he'd shut me out. Shut us all out, like some kind of angry snapping turtle that had bitterly retreated into its shell. Poke your finger too far inside and it might get bitten off. I'd never seen Marty so enraged.

I was scared for him.

I changed the subject. The whole conversation was getting way too deep for me.

"What do you even do?" I asked, wondering how he made a living. I mean, I knew nothing about his job, where he lived, what his favorite movies were. He was a total stranger to me, a complete foreigner who was now just randomly popping into my life from totally out of nowhere.

And just because he popped, did that mean I had to let him? *Sheesh*, if smoking weren't such a revolting, terrible, gives-you-cancer habit, I think I wouldda needed a cigarette.

"I make chips," he answered.

"Like potato chips?"

"No." He smiled. "Computer chips. For smartphones, mobile media devices, tablets. I tinker for a living."

"Are you rich?"

"I do okay," he said. "The business changes very fast, though."

"I need to go to bed now. Got some big stuff tomorrow."

"Yeah, your mom told me. Academic something or other," he said. "Mind if I come?"

Huh?

"You know, to root you on?"

'Cause, like, that's what dads do, right? They root their kids on. Pah-thetic.

"Whaddya think?" he asked. "I'd like to sit in the audience and support you, if that's okay."

No, it wasn't okay. I didn't want him to come. But then again, I didn't want to be a bad person for not wanting him to come, either. I mean, when I think of Q, I know she'd chop off her left leg to have her dad sitting in the audience to "root her on," but she would never have that opportunity again.

Wow, I must be a real jerk. However, I also didn't have any fun pictures of me and my father wearing matching Mickey Mouse ears, either. And I hadn't even gotten a stupid birthday card from him for the past eight years. But now he wanted to sit in the audience while I answered questions meant for Harvard brainiacs, as if we were some sort of warm, fuzzy, lovey-dovey TV family like you'd see in a baby-shampoo commercial?

Urrggh, why did all of this have to be so confusing? And so stressful? Couldn't he just disappear again?

No. I do not want you to come.

"Whatever," I said. "It's a free country."

Note to self: gotta work on saying what I'm really thinking before I reach adulthood.

"Actually, tickets cost fifteen dollars," he told me. "Some kind of community fund-raiser."

"You already bought one?" I asked. He didn't answer. Big on assumptions, wasn't he?

"Just determined to fill some holes, dimps. Just trying to fill some holes."

Far as I was concerned, that was enough hole-filling for one night, so I rose from my chair and headed for my bedroom. Forget the apple. Not eating it would only mean I might lose another two ounces before I hit the stage tomorrow, and if TV cameras really did add ten pounds, that meant they would really only be adding 9 pounds 14 ounces, because there are 16 ounces in a pound, and when you convert to the metric system you have to remember that there are 2.2 kilometers to every mile, but a meter is somewhat close to a yard.

My head was spinning with Septathlon information. Goodness, I needed rest.

"Okay, so, I guess I'll, umm, see you tomorrow?" he said. "And good night?"

I wasn't sure if he expected a hug or something, but whatever; he wasn't getting one from me.

"Yeah. G'night."

I grabbed my backpack and headed for my room. However, on the way there, I heard Mom step out into the dining room to ask my dad a question, so, like any good kid, I ducked behind a wall and eavesdropped.

"How'd it go?"

"Slow," he responded. "Very slow"

"You expected different?"

"I'd hoped."

"Well, you did all this to yourself," Mom said in a stern tone.

"I know," he answered softly. "I know."

My mom, her sixth sense of motherliness apparently tingling, must have suspected something, and a moment later she craned her neck to look around the corner.

Busted!

Thump, thump, thump. I darted to my bathroom, turned on the tub, and quickly started getting undressed. A few moments later, there was a tap at the door.

"Knock, knock, Boo...Can I come in?"

I put on my bathrobe. After all, I was far too ashamed of my body to let even my mother see me undressed these days. Kiki Masters I was not.

I unlocked the door. "Come on in."

Mom entered and smiled warmly. Her brown hair swayed to the left as she sat on the edge of the tub and gently checked the temperature of the bath.

"How you doing, honey?" she asked.

"'Kay," I said.

She paused, waiting for more. Mom knew me too well, better than anyone, probably.

"Boo, come on. What's up?"

"I'm worried, Mom. Worried about you. This whole thing's weird. He's weird."

"He's not weird."

"Okay, he's not weird," I conceded. "I mean, it's not like he has three nostrils or anything, but still, it's weird, ya know? I mean, you're, like, dating Dad."

"Yeah," she said. "I am."

I had a feeling he might have been right outside the door, trying to listen in on our conversation, but the tub was still filling with water, and hearing our voices over the noise was probably impossible.

Still, I talked low.

"What's this about, Mom?"

"About?"

"Yeah, like, what are you doing? What do you want?"

"Want?" She didn't really seem prepared for the question.

"Yeah," I said. "Like, what do you want?"

She ran her hand back through the rising bathwater.

"I'm not sure," she said. "Actually, I know what I want," she added, as if suddenly realizing she'd known the answer all along. "I want what's best for my kids."

"Not what's best for you?" I asked.

"Aw, Boo, when you're a mom, you don't really think like that."

"But you should," I told her. "You should think about you, Mom. You need to do what's right for you, not just me."

She stared at me, her eyes getting watery.

"Thanks, Boo. You're the best."

She took a bottle of rosemary-mint bubble bath down from the shelf and poured some into the water. A cloud of freshness filled the room.

"Your tub's ready," she said, moving her hand gently through the foam. "You want me to . . . you know, wash your hair?"

"Aw, Mom," I said as she turned off the water. "I wash my own hair these days."

She smiled, and a tear fell from her eye. "I know you do, Boo. I know you do." She stood and kissed me on the forehead. "Get some rest tonight, honey. I'm proud of you."

"Proud of me?" I said. "For what? I haven't done anything."

"Boo, you do more for other people than I think you'll ever know."

She wiped the tears from her eyes and walked out. I reached over, locked the door again, and got in the tub. The warm water felt soothing, nice. I dunked my head, put a washcloth over my eyes, and tried to let all the stress melt away.

Sometimes, there's nothing better than a warm bath with yummy smells.

At lunchtime, the six of us met in the campus courtyard to sort out some last-minute details about the competition later that night. We gathered on the ThreePees' turf, right by the brick wall near the cement stairs. As nerds, Beanpole, Q, and I usually sat in the far end of the courtyard, away from everybody. As the pretty, popular, perfect petunias, the ThreePees sat in the middle of everything.

That was just the way life worked. The best-looking people with the best-polished fingernails got the best lunchtime real estate. Everyone else got the leftovers. No use complaining.

It was funny how joining the ThreePees at their table felt weird to me, as if I'd entered an area where I instinctively knew I didn't belong. It was strange, because no one really "owned" the lunch area; the school did. But the way kids always divided it up in the same way, year after year, it was practically a tradition, one that had probably been formed way back before I was even born. Kids just followed the same pattern: cool kids in the center, everyone else everywhere else.

The unspoken rules of life were so bizarre, when I really thought about them. I wondered, was I the only one who wasted brain waves thinking about this kind of stuff?

Q, Beanpole, and I sat down. People showed up for the giant end-of-the-year Graduation Groove Down or the Love Is in the Air Valentine's Day soirée. But no one on campus really gave two scoops of a poop about the Academic Septathlon. And for sure, not a soul at Grover Park planned on coming out to support us at the Civic Center. I didn't blame them, though. Heck, if I hadn't had to be there, I would have stayed home and twiddled my thumbs, too.

The talk of the town we were not.

"All right, let's draw numbers for the order we'll appear in," Kiki said, taking out a pen and a sheet of paper. "I mean, it's ridiculous we haven't figured this out already," she added, with a disapproving look at me.

"Ooh," Sofes asked. "Can I pick first?"

"You can't pick at all," Brattany said. "She's only writing down five numbers, not six."

"Yeah, Sofes," Kiki told her. "We already decided that you're going last, remember?"

"But I thought that was a joke," Sofes said.

"The only joke is that you're even going to be onstage with us." Kiki wrote down the numbers one through five down on a sheet of paper. "Hopefully, by going last, you'll get less questions than the rest of us. Every point could count."

Beanpole, Q, and I didn't say anything on behalf of Sofes, as

Kiki, having written down the numbers, began tearing the sheet of paper into five little strips to be folded over. Clearly, Sofes's feelings were hurt. Clearer still, though, was the fact that Kiki and Brattany really didn't give a hoot.

"All right," Kiki said, mixing up the numbers. "Pick, dorks."

She held out her cupped hands with the five pieces of paper that would determine our order of appearance. Once this was decided, it would be set, no changes. In a world of rules, rules, rules, everything in the Academic Septathlon was predetermined.

We picked. The order in which we would appear turned out to be:

1. Beanpole
2. Brattany
3. Me
4. Kiki
5. Q
6. Sofes

"There. Now for the captain," Kiki said, giving me another look. "I guess we'll just have to flip a coin."

"Or you could just let—" Q paused to cough. She looked even paler today. "You could just let Maureen be captain."

"Is the Alien Answer Machine even going to live to see the end of this?" Brattany asked.

"Yeah," Kiki said. "She looks like her home planet is calling."

"You know, I think it'd be nice if we stopped calling one another names," Beanpole interjected. "After all, we're teammates. We need to embrace our oneness."

"All I'm saying is that I better not catch something from her," Brattany replied. "My dad's a lawyer."

"Just flip the coin," I said, thanking the heavens this would end soon enough.

Brattany took a quarter out of her purse. Q inspected it to make sure that it actually had two sides and wasn't one of those rigged thingamajiggies that allowed the coin flipper to cheat. Knowing the ThreePees, I wouldn't have put it past them.

Satisfied that everything was legit, Q passed the coin back to Brattany, who got ready to make the toss.

"Call it in the air, Kiki."

"Why does Kiki get to"—*Cough-cough*—"call it?" Q asked.

"It's okay," I said, not really caring either way. "Let's just get this over with." I didn't want to mention it, but I had to pee.

"Kiki...call it." Brattany flipped. The coin sailed high in the air.

"Heads!" Kiki cried. We stared as the coin hit the ground.

"Tails. Maureen is"—*Cough-cough*—"captain."

Kiki slammed her hand down on the table.

"Two out of three," Brattany suddenly said.

"No way," Q exclaimed. "That's such bunk."

"It's always two out of three on planet Earth, allergy girl," Brattany replied.

"Then you should have"—*Cough-cough*—"said that," Q replied.

"Whatever," I said to Q. "Just let's finish this, already. G'head, flip it again."

Brattany smiled at Kiki with a kind of *Don't worry, I got your back* look in her eyes as she got ready to flip the coin a second time.

"Kiki, call it in the air."

"Again, she gets to call it?" Q asked.

"Just flip it," I said. I didn't even want to be captain. The only reason I was putting up a stink about it was that Kiki did want to be captain, and any wrench I could throw into her life seemed like a good wrench for me to throw.

Come to think of it, throwing a wrench at her head didn't seem like a bad idea, either.

"Come on, Keeks," Sofes cheered. "You can do it."

"I can do what?" Kiki asked.

"You can win it!" Sofes replied exuberantly.

Kiki flashed her a look of scorn. "You do realize that there is nothing I can actually do right now, don't you, Sofes? I mean, the coin gets tossed in the air and then we watch to see how it lands. There really is no *doing*."

"Well," Sofes replied. "If there was doing, you could do it."

"Whut-ever," Kiki said dismissively.

"Call it, Kiki."

"This is such bunk," Q grumbled. "It was never supposed to be two out of three."

"Put a sock in it, nerd. Here we go." Brattany flipped the coin. Kiki's eyes grew wide with hope.

"Tails!" she bellowed. The coin landed.

"Heads. Maureen's our captain," Q announced.

Kiki slammed the table again.

"Unless you want to go three out of five. Or maybe five out of sev—" Q began to cough, unable to finish her sentence. She reached for a swirly-straw sip of her brown sludge, but not even that seemed to help.

"You sure you're not going to flurb out on us, freako?" Kiki snipped. "I mean, that would be such a nerdwad thing to do."

Q, because of her coughing, couldn't respond.

Brattany shook her head as Q struggled to catch her breath. "I'm warning you," Brattany said, pointing at Q. "My dad's a lawyer."

"I'll"—*Wheeesh-whooosh. Wheeesh-whooosh*—"be there," Q finally answered after a slurp on her inhaler. "Bet on it."

"You know, we'd be a much better team if we actually supported one another in our oneness."

"Just do us a favor and worry about yourself, Beanpole," Kiki replied. "And be on time tonight. TV shows always start on time."

"Yeah," Brattany added. "Six o'clock on the boob tube, which means officially signing in by five thirty, or we're automatically disqualified."

"Don't you think we should meet at least thirty minutes earlier than that, like by five?" Beanpole asked. "For the uniforms and stuff."

"Fine," Kiki replied. "But my advice," she said, staring at Q, "is bring a stretcher for the creature. She looks like she's going to need an ambulance to get her to the stage."

"Keep talking, witch, and I'll—" Alice stopped, coughing and wheezing harder.

"So dismal," Kiki scoffed.

Our business in the prime real estate section done, Beanpole and I led Q back to our usual lunchtime spot.

"Are you okay?" I asked Q, when we finally got to our table.

"Fine," she answered, pushing me away.

"But maybe you should—"

"I'm fine, Mom," she replied sarcastically. Clearly, Q was sick and tired of the way people were always asking about her health. "Don't you gotta"—*Cough-cough*—"go pee or something?"

"Actually—"

"Then don't let me"—*Cough-cough*—"keep you."

I turned to Beanpole for support. "You don't see any cause for concern here?"

Beanpole shrugged. "She's got a doctor. I mean, it probably just looks worse than it is."

"Looks worse than it is. She looks like a zombie." I turned to Q. "No offense, of course."

She stuck her tongue out at me.

Q was chilled yet sweating, her hair damp, sticking to the sides of her neck. A part of me felt like I should call her mom right away, but another part of me knew that if I did, Q wouldn't speak to me for the next two hundred years.

If even then.

I shook my head, picked up my backpack, and got ready to head to the restroom.

"For the record, I think you should go to the school nurse," I told her.

"And for the record, I think you should go to—" Her cough prevented her from finishing her thought, but I had a feeling I knew what she had been about to say.

I walked away. *Sheesh,* she is so hardheaded. I mean, being stubborn is one thing, but being an absolute—*oomff,* I bumped into somebody before I could finish my thought.

"Excuse me," I said.

"Hey, Maureen."

I looked up at the person I'd just crashed into. It was Logan Meyers, the blond-haired, blue-eyed Greek god of middle school.

"Oh hey, Logan. Sorry, I was just thinking about something."

"Watchya doin'?" he asked.

"Um, going to the restroom," I responded.

"Restrooms are stupid."

"Uh, yeah…" I said, at a loss for words. "Excuse me." I began to walk past him.

"I was gonna come tonight."

I stopped.

"To the Civic Center?" I said.

"Yeah," he answered. "I mean, Civic Centers are stupid, but I wanted to, you know, support you."

"You did?"

"Actually, I'll probably fall asleep," he confessed. "Unless they let me play video games on my phone. Video games are not stupid, you know."

"Wait," I said, uncertain. "Like, you bought a ticket?"

"Uh-huh." He smiled, his blue eyes shimmering like the Pacific Ocean. "But I gotta say, fund-raisers are stupid."

Suddenly, I heard a familiar voice from over my shoulder. "Well, well, well, if it isn't one of the proud members of our Grover Park Academic Septathlon team." There was no need to turn and see who it was. The tone was too recognizable. "So, are we excited about tonight?" asked Mr. Piddles.

"Uh, yes, sir," I said. What part of this whole experience hasn't been a unique and memorable joy? I thought.

"Funny," Mr. Piddles commented, looking around. "I haven't seen much of your coach lately."

"Really?" I said, as if this were the craziest comment I'd ever heard. "Oh, he's been working us so hard."

"Has he, now?" Mr. Piddles asked, his teacher eyes lasering in on me. Those eyes, they were like truth beams, the kind that could read my soul. I got flustered and decided to hightail it out of there.

"If you'll excuse me, I have to use the restroom."

"Of course, shirking one's professional duties would not be what I'd call very just, now, would it, Maureen?"

Gulp. I knew I was about to get trapped into revealing something if I dared to open my yapper, so I lowered my head, pretended the comment didn't require any response, and got ready to make a beeline for the girls' bathroom.

But, of course, not talking was almost the same as talking, because it told Mr. Piddles I was hiding something. That was all he needed to confirm his suspicions.

"When you are done, Maureen, I'd like to see you in my classroom, please," Mr. Piddles said. "And don't worry about attending your next class. I'll write you a pass once we are through with our discussion."

Ah, jeez, I thought, I can't win for losing. I moped off to the bathroom.

"Like, see you tonight, Maureen!" Logan excitedly called out.

"See ya, Logan."

"Perhaps one day you'll try out for an academic club, Mr. Meyers?" Mr. Piddles said to Logan as I walked off.

"No offense, sir," Logan replied, "but putting me on a team like that, well, it would be kind of stupid."

I could tell by the fact that Mr. Piddles didn't answer that he might have actually agreed with Logan on that one.

I pushed open the door to the girls' restroom, a bunch of thoughts swimming through my mind. Logan was coming to support me? I was being summoned to Mr. Piddles's room to talk about the coach who wasn't really our coach? Q wanted me not to get involved in doing anything about the fact she looked ready to hurl up her endocrine system? *Sheesh*, couldn't a kid just take a pee without so much drama?

I disappeared into the stall, feeling as if my bladder were about to burst. But when I finally sat down, nothing happened.

I tried to concentrate. *Oh, come on, come on*, I said to myself. I had to pee so bad I couldn't even do anything. *Sheesh*, I hated when that happened.

Then, a moment later... *Ahhhhh.*

What gives more relief than a good tinkle?

By 4:15, Beanpole and I had shown up at Q's house dressed in our Aardvark uniforms, ready to head out to the Civic Center. Q, however, was locked in the bathroom.

"She's not feeling well," Mrs. Applebee informed us. "And she's not going."

Not going?

The door flew open. "I'm fine!" If Q hadn't been sporting the complexion of a seasick earthworm, I might have agreed with her. "And I am going. Be ready in a sec."

"You are going nowhere, young lady."

"Mom, I'm healthier than you think." Q pushed her way past the three of us. "Everyone is counting on me," she said as she zipped into the bedroom. "Dressed in a minute."

Bam! The door slammed shut, the hallway silent.

"She doesn't look so good," I said softly.

"She's a tiger," her mom explained, a look of great concern

on her face. "Takes after her dad that way." Mrs. Applebee checked her watch. "And once she gets fixated on something, there's just no talking to her."

Uh, hello, welcome to my world, I thought.

Neither Beanpole nor I said anything as Q's mom debated what to do. "We've been fighting for the past several... I don't even know how long now," she informed us. "She thinks I hover too much, but she's not well." She checked her watch again, then picked up her purse. "I'll get the car started and meet you girls out front. If I know Alice, she's going to be there tonight even if she has to swim through a lake of alligators to do so."

Shaking her head with a look of *I must be nuts to permit this*, Mrs. Applebee went out the door that led to the garage. I turned to Beanpole with a *Should we do something?* look in my eyes. No, Q wouldn't listen to her mom, but she might listen to us.

Beanpole looked up from her cell phone, where she'd been tapping away, and shrugged. "You know there's no way that Alice is not going to prove to her mom that she's capable of taking care of herself."

"But where'd she get this crazy idea from, anyway?" I asked.

"From you."

"From me?" I said.

"Uh-huh," Beanpole replied. "When you started to believe in her earlier in the year, she started to believe in herself."

What?

"Oh, great," I said. "Now I'm inspiring people. Tell me, has this world become so pathetic that I'm some sort of shining light?"

"Guess so, Captain," Beanpole said with a smile.

"Don't call me that," I said. "I mean, it's not like any real responsibility comes with the title, anyway."

The door to the bedroom flew open, and Q appeared, blazing with strength in her Aardvark uniform, her facial features looking as if she'd just been exposed to nuclear radiation.

"Ah, my prize pupil," I said.

"Come on," she responded matter-of-factly. "Let's go."

"Are you sure you don't want to bring some peanuts for the road?" I asked. "Or perhaps gulp down another jug of cashew sludge? What about an almond butter–macadamia nut milk shake covered with pecans, walnuts, and pistachios? I mean, it seems only fitting, doesn't it?" My sarcasm was too clear for her to miss.

"Oh, there is one thing," she said.

"Yeah?" I asked. "What's that, Q?"

"There are no definitions provided in the Academic Septathlon, so no need to ask."

"There aren't?" Beanpole replied, rattled by the news.

"Don't worr—" Q began to cough. "Don't worry, Barbara. You'll be fine."

"Wait," I said. "When did you find this out?"

"The first day," Q answered.

"You mean to tell me that for the past few weeks you've known that a contestant can't ask for a definition, and yet you're just telling us this now?" I asked. "Why?"

"It made you funny like a cartoon." She grinned and raised her inhaler. *Wheeesh-whooosh. Wheeesh-whooosh.*

"Okay, so if what your eating doesn't poison you, just know that after this whole thing is over, I am going to make you a nice warm bowl of rattlesnake-venom soup." Q's grin grew larger. "I can't believe that this whole time you've just been messing with me."

"Aardvark. Seventeenth time."

"Come on, guys," Beanpole said, looking at her phone. "We'd better go. There's traffic."

The three of us exited the house. I shook my head in disbelief. "You're like the nerdwad of the century," I said, but the truth was, I felt better. I mean, if Q's sense of humor was still intact, that sort of meant she wasn't going to croak, didn't it? Of course, I wanted to murdalize her, but how was that different from almost any other day?

Q jumped into the front seat, Beanpole and I jumped into the back, and we all clicked our seat belts shut.

The look of disapproval on Mrs. Applebee's face was too obvious to miss.

"Nerd Mobile, onward," Q directed.

Mrs. Applebee glared at her daughter. Q didn't make eye contact with her, though. Instead, she stared straight ahead, prepared for another standoff.

"Um, Mrs. Applebee," Beanpole said, staring at her phone, "I don't think you should take Highway 4 to the Civic Center."

"What, she's going to take the back way and go down Seventeenth Street?" I asked sarcastically. "That's, like, two or three extra miles and another ten to fifteen minutes, with the stop signs. We're already late."

"I trust my trusty phone." Beanpole said, turning her cellie around to show me. "And it says the highway's jammed."

I looked at the map. Where there was bad traffic, the roadway on the screen was red. Highway 4, however, was not just red; it was red and black, with stripes and a big exclamation point in the middle, which could only mean one thing:

An accident. A bad accident.

"Whaddya think?" Beanpole said.

I checked the time on my phone. It was already 4:43. "We'll be cutting it close."

"But if we take the highway, we might not make it at all," Beanpole replied. "And Seventeenth Street is pure green right now, no traffic at all," she added, proudly holding up her phone. "Let's vote. Who says the back way? Raise your hand," she said.

And then, to show her enthusiasm for taking the back way, Beanpole's hand screamed to the sky. "I vote for . . . *Ouch!*" She smashed her wrist into the roof. "Don't worry, don't worry, I'm okay." Beanpole cradled her arm. I swear I thought I'd heard a bone crack. "Remind me to try and remain at one with the universe, accepting things as they are today, okay, Mo? I'm a little excited right now."

"Whatever you say, Nerdy Lama."

"Back way," Q chirped, casting her vote. Slowly, I nodded in agreement.

"Okay, back way it is," Mrs. Applebee said. "Assuming we should even be going in the first place."

"Which we should," Q replied.

After another shake of her head, Mrs. Applebee began to drive, and we set out for the Civic Center, making it just in time.

And when I say just in time, I literally mean just in time. We walked through the doors at 5:26. Kiki looked as if she were about to have a heart attack. She frantically waved us up to the registration table, and we scurried over to meet her.

"Grover Park Aardvarks, all here," Kiki said breathlessly to the seated woman. As it turns out, the lady in charge of officially verifying the registration of each of the Academic Septathlon participants was also the Supreme Judge of the night's proceedings. Her name was Miss Terrier, a woman in her fifties who was as thin as a rail and dressed in a smart, conservative, bluish-gray business suit. Her small glasses and pointy nose made her look like some kind of cross between a Harvard PhD and an evil stepmother from a terrifying fairy tale. "Quick, give her your papers," Kiki instructed.

"What papers?" Beanpole said, a puzzled look on her face. Kiki froze.

"Ha-ha, just kidding." Beanpole pulled out the official forms and handed them to Miss Terrier. "We're the Aardvarks," she said, perky and proud. "Nice to meet you."

Miss Terrier glanced at the clock sitting on the registration desk in front of her.

5:28.

"I'm charmed." Miss Terrier took our paperwork. We watched anxiously as she looked over the rim of her glasses to inspect our forms, making sure every *i* was dotted and each *t* was crossed. A quiet panic flooded through me as I prayed that none of us had been careless enough to have missed a line or forgotten a signature.

I think it was Miss Terrier's hair that most made me nervous. She wore it in the tightest bun I'd ever seen, not a single strand out of place. It was as if even her follicles knew they had to follow the proper rules and procedures, or they'd be dealt with in the most severe manner.

After what seemed like ten thousand hours of formal form inspection, Miss Terrier took out a red stamp and punched our documents.

"Grover Park Aardvarks, check," she said, putting our papers in the black tray to her left. "Wait there, please."

Phew, we made it. We walked over to the spot Miss Terrier had pointed to, near the other teams by the stage door.

"What on God's green earth took you dorks so long?" Kiki asked as we headed to our designated waiting spot. "Another two minutes and we'd have been disqualified."

"There was traffic," I said.

"You should have left earlier," Brattany said.

"We made it, didn't we?" Q said through a cough.

Kiki and Brattany took notice of Q's condition and stared at her with semihorror on their faces, as if she had the plague or something.

"If you were so worried, why didn't you text us?" I asked, trying to draw attention away from Q's appearance.

"I don't want any of your nerd numbers in my phone," Kiki said.

"Yeah, it might lead to further communication once this thing is over, and that's the last thing we want," Brattany said with a sneer.

"Oh, yeah?" I said. "Well, what if I told you that—"

"Can we not argue for a minute, please?" Beanpole interjected. "I mean, we're here, we're looking good in our uniforms, and we're ready to break out some Aardvark whomp-'em powder. Come on, let's do a cheer.

> *"We're the Aardvarks,*
> *The mighty, mighty Aardvarks!*
> *We're the—"*

"Can the rah-rah stuff, Beanpole," Kiki interrupted. "I'm still not over the heart attack you almost gave me."

"Yeah," Brattany said. "I mean, just look at that."

We turned around and saw the Gilded Gophers from Evanton Middle School racing up to Miss Terrier's table.

"Made it," said their coach.

"No, you did not." Miss Terrier pointed to the clock on her desk.

"Oh, come on," the coach replied. He was a plump, balding man dressed in a green shirt with a yellow tie. "There was a motorcycle accident on the highway. What were we supposed to do?"

"I do not dictate the regulations, Mr. Harper. I merely enforce them," Miss Terrier responded. "Rules are rules, and five thirty was the deadline."

I looked at the time on my cell phone: 5:33.

"But it's not fair," one of the students pleaded.

"You can't be serious," said another.

The Gilded Gophers were from a charter school on the east side of town, and they had come in second place the past three years in a row. This year, however, their team was filled with veterans of the Academic Septathlon, and if anyone was expected to challenge Saint Dianne's for the regional championship, it was the kids from Evanton.

"Have a heart, Miss Terrier," Mr. Harper pleaded.

"Heart has nothing to do with it," Miss Terrier responded. "Rules dictate my actions, Mr. Harper. Nothing more, nothing less."

Suddenly another team raced through the side doors—the Townsend Owls—and rushed up to the sign-in table with panicked looks on their faces.

Miss Terrier, without a hint of emotion on her face, directed her eyes toward the clock on her desk.

The coach of the Owls glanced at the coach from Evanton. She could tell by the look on Mr. Harper's face that the Gophers had just been ruled ineligible. Same motorcycle accident. Same traffic to the Civic Center. Same reason for her school being late.

She lowered her head, knowing, without having even spoken a word, that her team, despite all its hard work and long hours of preparation, had just been ruled ineligible. Wordlessly, she turned to her students.

A brown-eyed girl with a ponytail began to cry. Then another student started to weep. A boy punched the air. Seeing the hurt on the faces of these kids felt like a steak knife in my heart, especially since it was a result of something completely unpreventable.

However, the pain I felt for them was clearly not a pain that was being felt by anyone else in the hall. One look at Wynston Haimes showed that. She was smiling and snickering with her teammates. After all, with Evanton out of it, Saint Dianne's chances of continuing their unprecedented winning streak had just skyrocketed.

Wow, I thought. The Septathlon was cutthroat. Like, ugly cutthroat. I mean, where was the sportsmanship?

A third team came racing through the doors, victims of the traffic jam. There were supposed to be nine teams doing battle that night. The motorcycle accident had just cut the number down to six.

One of the coolest things about being backstage before any kind of giant show is peeking through the curtains to look out into the audience, without their even knowing you are able to see them. However, at the Civic Center it was even cooler, because backstage was high tech all the way, with video monitors and fancy-looking LED lights that controlled everything. From where we waited, we could see, via little television screens, the outer hall by the concession stand; the whole front of the stage; the entire backstage area, where the TV crew from the local-access channel were checking wires and setting up; and even the audience.

"Eww, look, that guy in the middle row just picked his nose," said some kid from Moore Middle School. "I'll bet you a Twix bar he eats it."

"You lose," said his friend, also from Moore. "He just stuck it under the seat."

"Hey, look, Mo," Beanpole said, pointing at a different screen. "There's your father."

It was my father. I watched as he made his way through the seventeenth row toward the center, where my sister, mother, and brother were sitting. My dad took the empty seat right next to my brother.

Marty looked up.

When he saw my dad, I could tell right away he was shocked and had no idea he would be here tonight. The look on my brother's face morphed into an instant scowl. Angrily, he rose from his chair and changed seats, moving to the other side of Mom, putting as much distance between himself and our father as he could.

Wow, even through the video screen I could see the rage boiling inside him.

"Any last words of advice for your team, Coach?"

I turned, startled by the voice. It was Mr. Mazer, the principal. Next to him stood Vice Principal Stone. Both of them wore coats and ties, looking all schoolly formal.

"Of course I do," Vice Principal Stone answered. "Just remember," he said to the six of us, "if you get eliminated early enough, my wife and I can go catch a movie."

Principal Mazer gazed quizzically at Mr. Stone.

"My girls and I, we always joke around like that," Mr. Stone explained with a chuckle.

We chuckled back.

"Oh," Mr. Mazer said, offering up a halfhearted chuckle of his own. "Well, it's almost showtime. Are the Aardvarks ready?

You look ready. I mean, without a doubt, you'll be the best-dressed team out there tonight."

Beanpole smiled a big and proud smile, and then, out of sheer enthusiasm, waved hello to a student from Rawlston Middle School. No, she didn't know the kid, but to Beanpole, what did that matter? She was friendly to everybody, at one with the universe.

However, Mr. Mazer's comment had upset me. I mean, even though the subject hadn't come up among me and Q and Beanpole, we had noticed when we first walked into the Civic Center that the ThreePees were wearing matching green barrettes that would sparkle under the stage lights.

And we nerds had conveniently been left out when it came to this fashionable add-on. I was instantly bitter. Especially after all that Beanpole's mom had done to make our team look so good. Beanpole noticed the barrettes, but being Beanpole, she just shrugged it off.

"We still look great, Mo. Don't make mountains out of molehills."

"I'd like to make *them* into molehills," I said. It was just such a low-class move, I thought.

"Of course, we didn't get quite the student-body support that some of the other teams have," Mr. Mazer continued as he looked around at all the different students backstage.

Boy, he could say that again. I mean, some schools must have had at least one hundred kids in the audience, belting out cheers, getting rowdy, causing a lot of ruckus to root for their classmates. Our team had zilch in terms of encouragement. Nine out of ten kids at Grover Park probably didn't even know that the Academic Septathlon was going on tonight.

"But the one student we do have in the audience seems to be trying to hold his own out there," Mr. Mazer added.

Huh? Mr. Mazer looked at the monitor. Saint Dianne's had a sea of navy-and-red-clad kids who were doing cheers that looked professionally coordinated. The Youngly Middle School Cobras had fans dressed in orange and black who were making some kind of hissing sounds. Grover Park had one kid—exactly one loony, bonkers, semidemented student who was standing up in the middle of the crowd screaming at the top of his lungs:

"Grover Park,
Not stupid,
Smart!
Grover Park,
Not stupid,
Smart!"

"Is that Logan Meyers?" Beanpole asked.

"What kind of cheer is that?" Brattany said, wrinkling her brow.

"Oh, he came to support me," Kiki said, batting her eyelashes. "Isn't that *sweeeeet*?" I rolled my eyes. "You know," she continued, "that's the kind of gesture that makes me think about taking him back."

"Vomit alert," I said through a fake cough.

Kiki glowered at me, but before she could say anything, the

lights in the hall blinked twice, then dimmed, like in a power outage.

"Hey, the five-minute warning," Mr. Mazer said. "I should get back to my seat. Oh, Mr. Piddles, you made it. Good."

"Wow," Mr. Piddles said as he approached. "You wouldn't believe the traffic."

"Don't worry," Mr. Mazer replied. "I saved you a seat."

"Wonderful," Mr. Piddles said. "It'll give us a chance to"—he paused and made eye contact with me—"talk." He gave me one of those famous laser-beam teacher stares.

I lowered my eyes.

"You know," he continued, "about some campus developments I have recently been told of . . ."

"Oh, joy," Mr. Stone remarked sarcastically. "Shop talk, after hours."

"Indeed, I do think it will be of interest to *you*, Mr. Stone," Mr. Piddles answered. "Highly so, in fact."

"I have no doubt," Mr. Stone replied, in an *I really couldn't care less* voice.

"Well, Aardvarks, we're off. Good luck out there," Mr. Mazer said. "We'll be rooting for you."

Vice Principal Stone, lagging behind as Mr. Mazer and Mr. Piddles headed off to take their seats, turned around in such a way that neither of his colleagues could see or hear him, and pointed at his watch.

"Moo-vie."

A moment later, he was gone.

"He's not nice," Beanpole said in a firm tone.

"Wow, you really roasted him with that one, Beanpole," I said. "I mean, that's almost go-wash-your-mouth-out-with-soap language, coming from you."

"So, what was that all about?" Kiki asked, hands on her hips.

"What?" I said.

"The look Mr. P. gave you."

Gulp. Over Kiki's shoulder, I spotted the door to the back-stage restroom.

"I have no idea what you're talking about. Now, if you'll excuse me, I have to pee."

Phew, I thought as I headed toward the bathroom. Avoided that one. I guess sometimes there *are* benefits to having a teensy bladder.

After a well-timed pee and a hand wash with pink bathroom soap, I returned to my group. However, my group wasn't where I had left it. While I was in the restroom, each of the schools had been placed in some sort of order by the back wall, all the coaches gone. Standing with the teams, to my surprise, were the judges. All three. There were two men, one tall and thin, one potbellied and wearing glasses, and of course, there was the chief, Miss "No Nonsense" Terrier.

"There's our captain," Kiki said as I walked up, bitterness clearly in her voice.

"Wrists?" Miss Terrier said to me.

"Huh?"

"We need to see your wrists," the tall judge said.

"We've had cheaters," the potbellied man explained as Beanpole pulled her long sleeves back down after having just gone through the inspection I was about to go through.

I held out my arms and pulled up my sleeves. "Nothing to hide," I said.

Satisfied, Miss Terrier turned to Q, the last in our group.

"And you, too, young lady."

Q, having already taken off her nonregulation calculator watch in the car and given it to her mom, pulled up her sleeves to prove she had nothing written on her arms.

"All clear," she said.

The judges nodded in approval.

"And that is?" Miss Terrier asked, peering at the oddly shaped item in Q's left pocket.

"A medical device," Q said, withdrawing her inhaler. "It meets all the criteria on page thirty-six, paragraph four, section two in the regulatory handbook."

Miss Terrier inspected the device.

"And yes, I have a doctor's note on file with school, should you need to"—Q began to cough—"should you need to verify."

The potbellied judge smiled. "Well, indeed, it is refreshing to have a contestant who's taken the time to familiarize herself with the rules."

Q grinned.

"*Knowing* the rules and *obeying* the rules are not the same thing," Miss Terrier noted as she slowly handed back Q's scuba tank. "Let's just hope that tonight your team doesn't confuse the two."

"I don't believe we will," Q answered. The two of them, Q and Miss Terrier, looked deeply into one another's eyes.

Is Q having a staring contest with the Queen of Mean? Like, OMG, is she crazy?

"Good," Miss Terrier replied, the first to blink. "Then you'll be sure to remember that once the competition starts, only the captain will be permitted to officially address the judges."

"Once the competition begins, we certainly will," Q replied. "But technically, it hasn't started yet."

"But technically, it's about to," Miss Terrier responded. "And I like technicalities."

Q took a slurp from her inhaler. *Wheeesh-whooosh. Wheeesh-whooosh.* "Me, too."

Again they stared at each other, eye to eye.

"Then mind them tonight, Grover Park," Miss Terrier said, "and good luck."

With that, Miss Terrier, her spine straight, her hair perfect, walked away, the two other judges following along closely behind.

"What are you doing?" I said to Q. "Trying to get her mad at us before we even begin?"

"I like her," Q answered as the judges inspected the wrists of another team.

"But it feels like she's ready to disqualify us at any moment," I said.

"I know," Q answered admiringly. "And she does it with such"—*Wheeesh-whooosh. Wheeesh-whooosh*—"style."

"You are weird," I said.

"Aardvark."

"Come on, girls," Kiki said to her two coconuts. "It's fire time."

"Fire time?" I asked as they began to walk away.

"Yeah," Kiki said, taking out her mascara. "Fire time. Probably not usually a big concern for you."

Brattany, lipstick in hand, smiled and got ready to inspect herself in a backstage mirror, while Sofes took out a hairbrush.

Armed with beautification tools of the kind that I didn't even own, the ThreePees wiggled off to make sure that they were, well... ThreePee enough for the cameras.

"Can you believe them?" I asked, turning to Q. "I mean, the barrettes weren't enough; now they need to—" I stopped in midsentence. "Are you running a fever?" I asked, noticing the sweat on Q's brow.

"Uh-huh."

"More than 101?"

"Uh-huh."

"More than 102?"

"Yup."

"More than 103?" I asked, my alarm growing.

"One-oh"—*Wheeesh-whooosh. Wheeesh-whooosh*—"five," Q said. "But that's only because I'm wearing this long-sleeved top."

My eyes practically popped out of my head. *One-oh-five?* I was so stunned I couldn't move.

"Don't worry," she said. "I've gotten up to 107 before."

Just then, the house lights dimmed again, but this time they didn't come back up to full brightness.

"Oh, relax, Mama Maureen, it's"—*Cough, cough*—"a manageable 101.8," Q said. "I'm fine."

"You're fine?" I said, taking in the greenness of her skin. "Let's not exaggerate, okay?"

"And here we go now," a guy in a black T-shirt barked at the teams as he adjusted a pair of headphones. "When I call your school, move to your assigned positions on the stage." He crossed over to the center of the big red curtain and listened for instructions from someone in a booth, probably in the rear of the auditorium. The ThreePees scurried back over, still tending to their looks.

"How's my lipstick?" Kiki asked Brattany, seeking a last-minute inspection.

"Dominating. Mine?" Brattany asked. Kiki took a moment to look over her teammate's lips, then adjusted a strand of her hair.

"Fierce," she said.

"Hey, turn your phones off, you guys, turn your phones off," Beanpole excitedly reminded us, waving her cellie. "Make sure they are powered *all* the way off, too. It's instant disqualification."

All six of us powered down our cells.

"Wait, like, um..." Sofes said. "Do I have to show my wrists every time I answer a question, or was that just a security measure like preventing terrorists from blowing up airports and stuff?"

"Just keep your answers short, Sofes," Kiki replied. "For the sake of all of us, keep your answers short tonight."

"Oh boy, here we go," Beanpole said, bouncing up and down with excitement. "Good luck, everybody."

She turned to the other teams that were waiting to head through the curtain and go out onstage.

"Good luck, you guys. Good luck. Have fun. Good luck."

She turned to Wynston Haimes. "Good luck."

"Kicking your butt will have nothing to do with luck tonight, sweetie," Wynston replied. "Nothing at all."

The girls from Saint Dianne's giggled.

"Rawlston, table one!" the stage manager yelled, holding the curtain open. The first kid from the Rawlston Rough Riders, a boy with gleaming silver braces, took a deep breath and walked out onstage. Instantly he was bathed in a flood of white light.

A burst of applause rose from the crowd. "Saint Dianne's, table two!" cried the stage manager.

"Ciao, Keeks," Wynston said as she approached the curtain.

"Eat glass, Wynston," Kiki replied. Wynston smiled with her jewelry-store-perfect teeth and led her team to their designated table on the stage, the crowd's energy growing more and more exuberant by the minute.

"Moore, table three!" yelled the stage manager.

With each team's appearance onstage, there was a new round of cheers and applause. "Youngly, table four. Danes Charter, table five."

Beanpole reached over and squeezed my hand, then Q's. "This is so fun," she said, her perk-o-meter once again cranked to its highest setting.

"Hey, why don't you lead us out, Beanpole?" I said.

"Me?" she replied.

After all, it was only because of her that our team looked so good, anyway.

"Why not?" I said. "I'm the captain. It'll be my first and probably only order of business tonight."

"Grover Park, table six."

Beanpole, her blood now screaming through her veins, stepped forward and walked proudly through the curtain.

But she missed the divide and got tangled up, caught like a fish in a net inside the long drapes. The guy in black rushed over before she could bring down the entire set of curtains, killing every contestant onstage, and pushed her through.

Beanpole, extracted from the red drapes, sort of stumbled out, nearly tripping as she emerged.

"Don't worry, don't worry, I'm okay," she said, her hair slightly messed up.

Ready or not, I thought as I prepared to step into the lights. It's showtime.

I walked through the curtain.

> *"Grover Park,*
> *Not stupid,*
> *Smart!*
> *Grover Park,*
> *Not stupid,*
> *Smart!*
> *G-o-o-o-o-o-o-o, Maureeen!!"*

"Ladies and gentlemen," came the silky-smooth voice of the announcer, "welcome to tonight's Region Eight Annual Academic Septathlon!"

ur master of ceremonies was a tall, sort of dashing middle-aged guy in a black tuxedo. I thought that was classy. However, every time he opened his mouth, he sounded like a cheesy game-show host.

"Hello, my name is Bingo Carter, and this very evening, tonight, right now, in just a few highly anticipated moments, we're going to strut our brains for your viewing pleasure. The stakes couldn't be higher, the tension couldn't be thicker, and the drama couldn't be more intensely intense."

"Intensely intense?" I said, turning to Q.

"My eyebrow's numb."

"Which one?"

"Both."

"Wow," I said. "This is intensely intense."

A banner hung over the edge of each table, identifying the

teams by the names of their schools. And really, what could make a person more proud than representing the Grover Park Aardvarks on national television?

Okay, it wasn't national television. But it was being live-streamed over the Internet at the same time it was being broadcast on channel 723, our local community arts station.

"Now, don't forget to donate," our host said to the cameras. "Fund-raising lines for Station 723 are open now. Tell them Bingo sent you."

Bingo's smile shone as if he had just waxed his teeth.

"Now, these teams have been studiously studying in order to prepare for the magical magic you are about to witness; the magical magic of"—music and sparkling lights whooshed through the auditorium as Bingo amped up the drama—"the Academic *Seepppttt*-athlon!" he boomed.

Strobe lights. A whirling spotlight. Pumping music. The special-effects guy must have pushed every button in the control booth.

For the most part, I never really watched TV. Thought it was stupid. But being *on* TV?

Way stupider.

"And that right there is what's known as the Circle of Inquiry," Bingo explained, referencing the podium inside a silver ring in the center of the stage. On the podium were two pencils, blank paper, and a microphone. Also, there was a monitor sitting on the floor, tilted upward so that the student would be able to read and reread the question once it had been asked. Of course, the audience could see the question, because on each side of the stage was a giant projection screen that beamed out everything that the TV audience was able to see at home.

Student pimples, bad haircuts, double chins (no names mentioned), the audience in the theater would be treated to it all.

"Each contestant, when it's their turn, will rise from their table, enter the Circle of Inquiry, and have forty-five seconds to answer one question," Bingo explained to the viewers. "It's a battle of brains. It's a battle of wits. It's a battle of battles!"

A battle of battles? I glanced over at the judges sitting downstage to our right. Even Miss Terrier rolled her eyes at that one.

"And now, let the magical magic begin!"

More strobe lights, pumping music, and whirling colors flooded the auditorium. Personally, I think the guy in the control booth must have gulped down too many espresso shots before he had come to work today. This guy was clearly caffeinated.

"Remember, phone lines are now open for donations," Bingo informed the audience. "Just call the toll-free number at the bottom of your screen, because, after all, what would life be without Station 723?"

Bingo's smile sparkled under the lights. For some reason, looking at him made me think of two words.

Restraining order.

"For the first question of the night, tradition dictates that we begin with our defending champions and then jump back in order. And so, from Saint Dianne's, you've seen them before...." A roar rose from a section of the crowd, the lights dimmed, and a spotlight shined on table number two. The girls from Saint Dianne's, dressed in their smartly cut skirts and well-tailored jackets, smiled for the cameras as if they'd practiced this moment a thousand times before.

"Send your first contestant down, it's time to do the *Seeppptttathlon!*"

Wynston Haimes, smiling like Miss America, high-stepped her way to the Circle of Inquiry with all the poise of a senator.

Bingo held up his note card and read the first question.

"The category is science.

"The trachea is part of the _____ system.
   a. digestive
   b. nervous
   c. cardiovascular
   d. respiratory
   e. anthropological"

Of course, Wynston nailed it. "D," she replied. "Respiratory."

"BINGO!" said Bingo. The audience cheered, and Wynston, smooth and refined, glided back to her seat.

Just like that, the game was on.

It was funny how the audience seemed to melt away almost immediately as soon as the questions started flying. Of course, with all the cameras and stuff, we couldn't forget we were on TV, but also, since the lights were so bright in our eyes, we really couldn't see the audience, either; we could just sort of feel them out there, which made focusing in on the questions a lot easier. Plus, I wanted to forget about the audience, anyway. With my hole-filling dad, my Darth Vader vice principal, my super-aggro brother, and all the strangers in the crowd who probably just saw me as the plump girl, I figured the sooner I put the audience out of my mind the better. Being onstage wasn't distracting; it actually let me focus and forget.

Things moved quickly as each of the students before us in round one got their answers correct. Truth is, I could have answered any of them, too. It seemed that the first round was loaded with easy stuff to build up our confidence.

I glanced up at the big, bright digital scoreboard.

SAINT DIANNE'S	5
RAWLSTON	5
MOORE	5
YOUNGLY	5
DANES CHARTER	5
GROVER PARK	--

"And last but not least, a team we haven't seen here in a while, the Grover Park Bulldogs."

Bulldogs?

"Say something," Brattany whispered.

"Yeah, you're the captain," Kiki added, an edge in her voice. Beanpole, Q, and Sofes looked at me.

I leaned into the microphone on our table. "Um, Aardvarks."

"Excuse me?" Bingo said, caught off guard.

"We're the Aardvarks," I said. "Not Bulldogs."

"Oh." Bingo looked at his note card. I could practically read his mind: *Must be a typo.* "Well, okay, little Aardvarks, why don't you show us what you've got? Who's going to be the first to bravely brave the Circle of Inquiry?"

Beanpole, having drawn the spot of number one back when we chose our team's order of appearance, headed for center stage. And she didn't fall, trip, slip, or collide with anything on her way there, either. Right then I should have known this was a sign that something was wrong.

"A day on Saturn takes about ten Earth hours.
Which fact would *best* explain this short day?
a. Saturn is less dense than Earth.
b. Saturn is much farther from the Sun than Earth.
c. Saturn rotates more rapidly than Earth.
d. Saturn's orbit has greater eccentricity than Earth's.
e. Saturn's planetary temperature exceptionally fluctuates."

An easy question, I thought.

"*B*," Beanpole replied. "The answer is *B*."

"Oh, I'm sorry, little Aardvark," Bingo said. "The correct answer is *C*."

A groan rose from the audience at the first missed question of the night. The digital scoreboard flashed the new scores:

SAINT DIANNE'S	5
RAWLSTON	5
MOORE	5
YOUNGLY	5
DANES CHARTER	5
GROVER PARK	0

"Nice going," Kiki said as Beanpole moped back to our table.

"I can't believe you bombed on such an easy one," Brattany added, with a shake of her head.

Beanpole looked at me, tears almost ready to fall from her eyes. "But I knew it," she said. "I just, I don't know, got nervous."

"It's okay," I told her.

"It's not okay," she replied. "I choked. I let us down."

"Listen to me, Beanpole," I said in a firm tone, noticing that Beanpole was about to go into the tank big-time. "There are a lot of questions yet to come. You studied hard, you're really smart, and we need you tonight, so let it go. You missed one. Big deal. We're all going to miss some before this thing is over," I said, glaring at Kiki and Brattany.

"Like heck, yeah, we are," Sofes confirmed, trying to be encouraging.

"No need to feel so proud about it," Kiki told her.

"Beanpole?" I said. "You with me?"

Beanpole raised her eyes. They were filled with woe-is-me sadness. But then the strangest thing happened. Her expression began to change. I watched as the dull look of self-pity shifted into a steely gaze of fiery determination.

"I'm with you, Captain," she confirmed crisply. "I guess I just forgot about my little bag of whomp-'em powder." Beanpole slapped an imaginary satchel as if she were carrying a mystical sack of magic Septathlon dust. "Next time, they're gonna taste some nerdvark pride."

"Okay, so, like, that's a little dorky for me to go with you on that one, but I'm glad you're feeling better." And clearly, she was, because the next time out—and the time after that—when it was

Beanpole's turn, she aced it. Sure, our team missed the first question, but after three rounds of competition, we weren't getting obliterated at all. In fact, we found ourselves in a tie for third place.

Saint Dianne's, of course, was practically a preprogrammed answer machine.

"Bingo!"

"Bingo!"

"Bingo!"

It seemed like every time they went to the Circle of Inquiry, Bingo said, "Bingo!" It wasn't long before they were running away with first place.

SAINT DIANNE'S	85
DANES CHARTER	50
GROVER PARK	40
MOORE	40
RAWLSTON	35
YOUNGLY	25

To everyone in the auditorium, it seemed as though the private-school girls with the SD crest on their smartly cut navy blue uniforms were going to easily cruise to the championship.

Until...

After a fifteen-minute intermission, a pee (I took two of them), and a chance to stretch our legs—a time during which Bingo must have made his fund-raising pitch of "Where would we be without Station 723?" to the camera a thousand times—the action resumed, and it was more of the same.

Saint Dianne's was creaming us. The real battle, as we could all see, was for second place. At least if you made it that far, you made it into the Ivy Zone, which was kind of like a superquiz round where the top two teams went head to head at fifteen points per question to see who'd be the grand champion. However, Saint Dianne's had built up such a large lead that even at fifteen points per question, it was almost impossible for another team to catch up.

Then Wynston's calculator died. Right in the middle of the Circle of Inquiry, while she was solving a math question.

She shook the machine a few times, but nothing happened.

"Batteries," she said, hoisting her calculator into the air for the judges to see. The potbellied judge nodded to her understandingly, and then Wynston went to her team's table, where she borrowed a calculator from a teammate and returned to the Circle of Inquiry.

"Seven sixteenths of a mile," Wynston said.

"Bingo!" said Bingo.

The next contestant, a boy from Moore, got ready to head to the Circle of Inquiry as Wynston returned to her seat.

Q nudged me.

"What?"

"You're the captain. . . . Speak."

"About what?" I said. "And by the way," I remarked, taking note of her complexion, "you're as green as a lizard."

"The calculator," Q replied, ignoring my comment. "The"—
Cough-cough—"calculator."

"What about it? Her batteries died." It annoyed me much more than I wanted to admit that Q was sweating and turning colors and looking as if she were about to morph into a zombie right in front of me. I mean, sure, I appreciated the fact that she had nailed five out of six of the questions she'd been asked—and she really was carrying our entire team. It didn't make any sense. I mean, hello, you've proven your point, now go home, cuddle up with your oxygenating hemoglobin thingamadoodle, and get into bed before you croak on live TV.

Arrgh, she was so frustrating.

"She broke the rules," Q told me. "What if her teammate did the problem and"—*Cough-cough*—"then left the answer on the screen when no one was looking?"

Hmm, hadn't thought of that.

"That's why there's a rule that says no borrowing," she added.

"And now," Bingo began, "for a historically based history question, we go to—"

"Excuse me," I interrupted, speaking into the microphone. "Excuse me, please."

Bingo stopped, startled by my interruption.

Miss Terrier quickly leaned forward to take control of the situation. "Yes?" she asked, a stern look on her face.

The spotlight swung around and made me the center of attention, practically blinding me with its brightness. I could feel every person in the auditorium staring at me.

"Um, the rules say you're not allowed to borrow."

"My batteries died," Wynston shot back in her own defense, speaking into the mike on her table.

"But how do we know that the screen was blank when the calculator was given to her?" I asked.

A gasp rose from the crowd. The spotlight moved off me and swung around to laser in on the girls from Saint Dianne's.

"That's not true!" Wynston exclaimed, fury on her face. "There wasn't anything on it."

"So let me get this straight," Miss Terrier said. "Are you accusing the team from Saint Dianne's of cheating?"

"No," I responded, shaking my head. I wasn't. I didn't think they were cheating. And I certainly wasn't the type of person who would lie and make up that kind of accusation just so I could win some stupid Academic Septathlon. "But rules are rules," I said, "and the rules say no borrowing."

A low buzz of murmurs and mumbles rolled through the crowd.

Miss Terrier leaned thoughtfully back in her seat and then huddled with the two other judges. Chattering voices began to fill the Civic Center as the judges deliberated. The girls from Saint Dianne's glared at me. If they had been given carving knives just then, I would have been sliced into sushi.

We waited as the judges considered what to do. The tall one flipped through the official rule book, looking up the bylaws, while the potbellied judge had a quiet discussion with Miss Terrier.

A moment later, they gave their ruling.

"The judges find," Miss Terrier said, "that yes, a violation has occurred."

A collective gasp burst from the audience. The section of the crowd that had been doing so much of the cheering was now on pins and needles.

Kiki, amped up with enthusiasm and unable to contain her

excitement, called across our table to me, "So they're disqualified?" The hopefulness in her voice that Wynston Haimes might get bounced on her butt from the competition in front of the entire universe caused her to practically shout her comment—and the microphone picked up every word she said.

Disqualified?

The idea sent an electric charge through the Civic Center. Every eye in the room rotated to Wynston Haimes, the violator. Immediately, her eyes got as big as dinner plates. Two minutes ago, she'd been planning a rub-everyone's-nose-in-it victory parade. Now she was on the doorstep of elimination and public humiliation. Panic appeared on her face.

"It's a class-three violation," Miss Terrier informed us, "an infringement that does not merit disqualification."

Phew. Wynston and the snobs from Saint Dianne's breathed the deepest sighs of relief I'd ever seen anyone ever take.

"But a penalty of seventy-five points will be deducted from their tally."

"Seventy-five points?!" Wynston cried.

Everyone looked at the scoreboard. It went from this:

SAINT DIANNE'S	135
DANES CHARTER	75
GROVER PARK	70
MOORE	60
RAWLSTON	60
YOUNGLY	55

to this:

```
DANES CHARTER          75
GROVER PARK            70
SAINT DIANNE'S         60
MOORE                  60
RAWLSTON               60
YOUNGLY                55
```

The audience exploded in chatter. A seventy-five-point deduction had taken Saint Dianne's from first place to third.

And Grover Park was suddenly in second. Without many more rounds to go.

A sense of chaos swept through the crowd as everyone in the audience tried to figure out what this new development meant for the team they were cheering for.

"Wow, those are some expensive batteries," Sofes said to Beanpole. "That's why, for my calculator, I only use sonar."

"Okay, everybody, settle down, settle down," Bingo said, trying to restore order in the audience. However, with all the kids from all the different schools still pointing at the scoreboard and trying to figure out their own team's chances, a new surge of liveliness had taken over.

"Come on, people, don't be a clown, settle it down."

With a line like that, Bingo wouldn't have lasted a single day as a middle-school teacher, I thought.

In the midst of all the commotion, however, amid all the noise, there was a calm and ruthless silence. It came from Wynston Haimes. She glowered at me from across the stage, the heat of her scowl practically burning a hole through my flesh.

The Academic Septathlon, I realized, had just become personal.

Let's be honest: up until the calculator debacle, the evening had been a total snoozer. With no drama, no team putting up a fight, and no one but Saint Dianne's raking up any significant points on the leader board, the audience must have felt like they were sitting in science class, when the clock was broken and the teacher just kept making them do problem after stupid problem from the boring textbook.

But once Saint Dianne's had had their score karate-chopped by the judges, it was GAME ON, and the crowd came alive. Every single question from that point forward mattered, and each school's cheering section grew louder and louder in support of their team.

> *"Go, SD, go!*
> *Go, SD, go!*
> *G-o-o-o-o-o, Strikers!"*

"Hey, hey, Moore,
    Show me what you got!
    Hey, hey, Moore,
    Show me what you got!"

A student from Danes Charter missed a toughie on the Industrial Revolution.

"Awwwww," came a groan.

I looked up at the scoreboard.

DANES CHARTER	90
GROVER PARK	90
SAINT DIANNE'S	85
MOORE	75
RAWLSTON	70
YOUNGLY	65

An hour and a half ago, who would have ever guessed that Beanpole would be in a position to answer a question that could put us in first place? Yet there she was, a shot at redemption at her fingertips after missing that first easy one.

Beanpole readied herself to head into the Circle of Inquiry.

"You okay?" I asked.

"Got my whomp-'em powder right here," she said, slapping an imaginary bag on her hip. With poise and confidence, she headed for center stage.

"Grover Park,
    Not stupid,
    Smart!

Grover Park,
Not stupid,
Smart!
G-o-o-o-o-o-o, Barbara!!"

Well, looky who's awake, I thought.

Beanpole turned to the audience, smiled, and even though she couldn't see him because of the lights, waved a big hello to Logan.

Continuing forward, Beanpole then turned back around to let us know she wasn't going to let our team down. With a grin of nerdish proportions, she gave our team a big thumbs-up.

And then she walked off the edge of the stage, falling face-first into the orchestra pit.

"Holy Sugar Puffs!" Bingo yelled, racing over to help her.

A moment later, Beanpole climbed back onstage, her hair a mess, her Aardvark shirt slightly torn at the shoulder.

"Don't worry, don't worry, I'm okay."

Sofes turned to me, seriously alarmed. "Shouldn't we go check on her?" she asked.

"For what?" I said. "That's how I know she's gonna nail this one."

And sure enough, when Bingo asked Beanpole what the significance was of the Appomattox Court House in relation to the U.S. Civil War, Grover Park banked another five points.

"*D,*" Beanpole answered. "It's where Robert E. Lee and the Confederates surrendered to the Union."

"Bingo!" said Bingo. "Well done, little Aardvarks."

The scoreboard flipped, and suddenly we were in sole possession of first place.

Beanpole cruised back to our table, her smile as big as a beach ball.

Sofes was the first to greet her. "Good job, Barbara!" she exclaimed, giving Beanpole a giant high five. They smacked hands with a perfect smash, the moment caught flawlessly by a cameraman.

I looked up at the big projection screen. The Grover Park high five was broadcast three times in a row to the audience, like one of those instant replays during the Super Bowl.

"Like I told you," Bingo said, looking into the camera. "Where would we be without Station 723? Donation lines are open now."

As soon as the camera was off our team, Kiki scowled at Sofes. "Don't do that," she said. "They're the enemy, remember?"

"But I thought *they* were the enemy," Sofes responded, looking over at Wynston and the team from Saint Dianne's.

"They're both the enemy," Kiki replied.

"Yeah," Brattany said, crossing her arms.

"Boy," Sofes commented, "we sure have a lot of enemies."

"It's the price of greatness, Sofes. The price of greatness."

Q shook her head, disgusted by Kiki's comments, and then coughed, her lizard green complexion evolving into full-blown iguana right in front of my eyes.

"Rawlston, come on down," Bingo said with great fanfare. "It's your turn in the Circle of Inquiry."

Every contestant onstage seemed to sense that the main

competition was getting ready to end, but in the Academic Septathlon, they never officially told you when you'd be moving on to the Ivy Zone superquiz segment of the contest, because they liked it to be a surprise. Thought that it kept all the teams trying as hard as they could and battling to the end or some stuff like that. But the questions were getting harder and harder, and Beanpole's correct answer turned out to be the last correct answer our team would get.

Even Q missed her next question. In fact, the only team that seemed to be answering any of the questions correctly was—guess who?—Saint Dianne's.

Suddenly, a bell we hadn't heard before—it sounded like an old car horn from one of those skinny-tire vehicles back when there were still horses and buggies on the road—blared through the auditorium.

"Well, guess what time it is?" Bingo asked. "That's right, it's time for the Ivy Zone."

"Oohh..." gasped the audience.

Once again, the hypercaffeinated guy in the control booth pushed every button he could get his hands on, and the Civic Center exploded into a flash of colored lights. I squinted to check out the scoreboard.

SAINT DIANNE'S	105
GROVER PARK	95
DANES CHARTER	90
MOORE	75
RAWLSTON	70
YOUNGLY	65

"It's going to be the Strikers of Saint Dianne's versus the little Aardvarks of Grover Park," Bingo announced. "And a contested contest I'm sure it will be. So won't you consider making a donation to our station? After all"—Bingo put on his best puppy dog face—"where would we be without Station 723?"

The lights onstage suddenly dimmed, and soothing elevator music began to play throughout the auditorium.

A lone spotlight shone on Bingo. He swaggered to the front of the stage and broke into song.

"The community arts
The local stage
The sound of a drum, the look of a child, an actor's
gaze..."

"I didn't know he could sing," Beanpole said as we stood in the near dark.

"He can't," I replied, ready to plug my ears.

"Over here, kids. You to that side, you to this side; let's go," the guy in the black T-shirt ordered as a group of technicians rushed from behind the curtains and began quickly rearranging everything in preparation for the Ivy Zone. By the time they were done, only two tables were left: ours and Saint Dianne's. Both had been moved closer to the Circle of Inquiry, while Bingo's singing kept the audience distracted.

"A tearful bow
Soliloquy
This amazing thing, 723, don't abandon me..."

"I don't think I've ever heard worse lyrics in my life," I said.

"Don't worry," Q replied. "I TiVo'd it so later on we can relive the joy."

On the other side of the stage, way far away from us, the girls from Saint Dianne's huddled and talked strategy. As team captain, was I supposed to huddle us up as well? For what? I thought. We'd already made it way further than we'd expected, and now I figured it was time to just go out and answer more questions. Plus, engaging in less conversation with Kiki Masters was always a good thing.

"You feeling okay?" I asked Q, checking in on her.

"Never better."

"You're a terrible liar."

"And you're a terrible friend," she replied. "I mean, I can't believe you made me come to this when—" She paused to cough. "Clearly, I should be home getting medical attention."

She took a slurp off her scuba tank—*Wheeesh-whooosh. Wheeesh-whooosh*—and smiled, then practically coughed up a gastric valve.

"Aardvark."

What could I do but smile?

"Aww, that's so sad," Beanpole interjected, her shoulders slumped. I turned and watched the kids from Danes Charter, Moore, Youngly, and Rawlston exit the stage. Behind the curtains, their coaches and parents greeted them with hugs and words like "Good job," or "We're so proud of you." But losing is losing, and there wasn't one kid walking off the stage who didn't want to be back on it.

And there wasn't one of us still standing on the stage who would have wanted to leave, either. This struck me as weird. I mean, the Academic Septathlon had been nothing less than an unwanted nightmare when we were first made to participate, but now that we were in the heat of battle, I had to admit, it was awesome. Who'd have guessed it, but I loved the pressure. I loved the challenge. I loved the feeling of being pushed and getting an answer right, even though, yep, it stung bad when I got an answer wrong.

But that edge, well... the adrenaline rush was so cool.

Most of all, however, I think I loved the fact that for almost the whole night, I'd stopped worrying. I'd stopped worrying about my dad; I'd stopped worrying about how the ThreePees always treated me; and, biggest shocker of all, I'd stopped worrying about how I looked. In the Academic Septathlon, it didn't matter how cute I was or how much my corduroys squeaked when I walked to the pencil sharpener; what mattered was who I was and how I performed. If only it could be that way for the rest of my life.

But, of course, it wouldn't. Tomorrow, life would go right back to being about clothes and hair and jeans size and who looked the hottest and whom you were dating and blah-blah-blah.

I'd never even been on a "real" date. Pah-thetic.

Bingo's voice boomed in a crescendo. This was going on YouTube for sure.

> *"Be true to me,*
> *723*
> *Think charity!!"*

"And we're back in five, four, three, two and one...." the guy in the black T-shirt said as he hustled our team over to the newly positioned tables onstage.

"Thank you," Bingo said to the audience, taking a bow. "Thank you very much." I didn't know why he was bowing and saying thank you to everyone. I mean, it wasn't like anyone was applauding.

"Well, looky here," Bingo continued, holding up a sheet of paper that had just been handed to him. "Seems the donations tonight are impressive. Keep it up, folks, and call the toll-free number on your screen right now. Just tell them"—he winked—"Bingo sent you."

"I think I'm gonna yak," I said.

"Me, too," Q replied.

"Be nice, you two," Beanpole said, scolding us. "I think he's talented."

"I wasn't kidding," Q said.

"Me neither," I answered.

"Ssshh," Kiki snipped. "A few more right answers out of you goons and we'll be living in the land of François Fumeil. Now, concentrate."

The team from Saint Dianne's walked up to their table in lockstep, arm in arm. Six girls, six navy blue blazers, six hateful glares.

"Good luck," Beanpole said, in an effort to be sportsmanlike. "May the best team win."

"We will," Wynston replied. "And deep down, you know it's going to happen, too."

Whoa, I thought. Someone should check for hair on this girl's chest.

"And now we enter through the entry of the Ivy Zone, the final round, which will bring finality to tonight's tournament. Strikers, are you ready?" Bingo asked.

The girls from Saint Dianne's nodded.

Bingo turned to us.

"Little Aardvarks, how about you?"

Why did he keep calling us little Aardvarks, I wondered.

"Yeah. Uh-huh. Yup," we said.

"Then let the magical magic *beeee*gin!"

Swirling lights. Another strobe. A roll of thunder. Personally, I think the caffeine buzz was wearing off for the guy in the control booth. I mean, the Ivy Zone explosion just didn't have quite the same pop as the ones from earlier.

"Each inquisition into your knowledge base will now be worth TRIPLE the points. Did Bingo just say triple? That's right, Bingo just said triple, making each correct answer now worth not five, not ten, but fifteen POINTS!"

I think Bingo expected some kind of hyperimpressed *Ooooh* to roll through the audience.

It didn't.

"And schools will now field two questions in a row, not just one per round. Strikers, send up the first of your next two contestants," Bingo instructed. He turned to the camera. "And it's all happening right here, live, on Station 723."

Note to self: be sure to get Bingo's celebrity autograph before leaving.

NOT!

Despite all the trumped-up drama, it was still the same contest: we went into the Circle of Inquiry, were given a question, and gave an answer. The multiple-choice aspect was gone, though; a student had to respond in her own words, without options being provided. Other than that, not much had changed.

And when I say not much had changed, I really do mean not much had changed. Saint Dianne's was still very good. However, I had to tip my hat to Kiki and Brattany, because, when it was their turn, they both nailed their questions. Then I missed one, but Beanpole got one right; then Saint Dianne's, shock of the century, missed two in a row, and Q got one right, while Sofes, yet again, got hers wrong.

"You're killing us, Sofes," Kiki said as Sofes walked back to our table from the Circle of Inquiry. "You're absolutely killing us."

"Come on," Brattany complained. "You gotta pull some weight. The way you're performing is, like, lamer than lame right now."

Sofes hung her head.

"Don't worry about it, Sophia," Beanpole told her. "You'll get 'em next time."

"I highly doubt it," Kiki replied.

"Yeah, with any luck, she won't even get a next time," Brattany added. "I'm sure this thing will be over soon."

"But we're still in it," Beanpole said, pointing to the scoreboard. And she was right. Even with Sofes laying an egg every time, we were more competitive than anyone expected us to be, and somehow, after thirty-five minutes of back-and-forth Ivy Zone questions, we were only fifteen points down.

SAINT DIANNE'S   195
GROVER PARK   180

Then the bell that sounded like a car horn blared again.

"You know what that sound means, don't you?" Bingo said. "It's the final showdown; just three more questions left, questions that will be worth"—he paused for dramatic effect—"TWENTY-FIVE POINTS APIECE."

The crowd still didn't *oooh*, but knowing that we were headed for the final face-off sent one last surge of energy through the auditorium.

"Strikers," Bingo said to the girls from Saint Dianne's, "you control your own destiny. Answer these next three questions and you are tonight's champions."

"Go, SD, go!
Go, SD, go!
G-o-o-o-o-o, Strikers!"

A student from Saint Dianne's named Zina stepped into the circle.

"The speed of a tuning fork's vibrations is known as its frequency. What is the unit of measurement used to assess this quantity?"

Zina lowered her head and spoke crisply into the microphone. "The quantity is measured in hertz."

"BINGO!" Bingo cried out.

Calista, the next girl up for Saint Dianne's, crossed to the Circle of Inquiry. Bingo read from his card.

"The nineteenth-century American policy of Manifest Destiny encompassed what political belief?"

"That, basically, the United States should be entitled to own all the land between the Atlantic and Pacific oceans."

"BINGO!" yelled Bingo. "And that means that if Saint Dianne's can answer this next question, they are guaranteed to win, and will repeat as champion."

Wynston Haimes, team captain, headed to the Circle of Inquiry. With elegance and certainty, she crossed her hands behind her back and listened intently.

"The category is Literature. . . .

"In the Bible, Adam and Eve were expelled from the Garden of Eden. Why?"

"Oh, my goodness," I said to Q. "I can't believe they just gave her the easiest question in the universe. This whole thing is rigged."

A big, cocky smile crossed Wynston's face. She took a moment to glare at me—and then at Kiki—in a smarmy, nasty way. A moment later, she leaned forward and spoke into the microphone.

"Because they ate the forbidden fruit of the apple from the tree of knowledge."

The girls from Saint Dianne's prepared to leap victoriously into the air.

"Oh, I'm so sorry, that is not correct," Bingo said. "It's because God did not want them to eat from the tree of life. Genesis 3:22–23; always a tricky one, huh?"

"Yes!" Kiki, exclaimed, pumping her fist.

"I think somebody might need to go back to Sunday school?" Bingo said in a good-humored way to the audience. "And that leaves the door open for the little Aardvarks to walk away with the trophy. But they'll have to go three for three to do it. Donation lines are now open."

I had to admit, I would have gotten that one wrong, too. But Wynston was the one who had gotten suckered, not me, and Grover Park had one last chance. Of course, we already knew the order in which we would have to appear, because we'd been through the lineup many times over. It was my turn first, Kiki's next, and Q's last. That meant that if Kiki and I could get our questions right, we'd be passing the torch to our cleanup hitter, Q, and really, who wouldn't have liked those chances? As everyone knew, she was our team stud.

I entered the Circle of Inquiry, took a deep breath, and focused.

> "Grover Park,
> Not stupid,
> Smart!
> G-o-o-o-o-o, Maureen!"

Logan's voice made me smile. Was I feeling the pressure? Oh heck, yeah. But was I having fun?

The time of my life.

I entered the Circle of Inquiry, and Bingo held up a blue note card.

"The category is History...."

"In the year 1215, this document was signed by King John of England, limiting the power of the ruler. Please name this document."

I leaned in to the microphone. "The Magna Carta."

"Bingo!" said Bingo.

"Yes!" I exclaimed with a pump of my fist. I walked back to our table.

"Nice job, skinny-chubby," Kiki said as she passed me on her way to the Circle of Inquiry. Even in my finest hour, she still had to twist the knife.

Whatever, I thought.

"Way to go, Mo!" Beanpole exclaimed. "Come on, Kiki, you can do it!"

"The category is Art...."

"In most mid-Renaissance paintings, the Virgin Mary is portrayed wearing the color blue. Please explain why."

"Because blue is a calm color, like, tranquil and pure and stuff."

"Bingo!" said Bingo.

Wynston grimaced. Kiki, class act that she was, turned to the girls of Saint Dianne's, puckered her lips and blew them a kiss. The team from SD scowled.

"Well, things are getting a little chippy out here as we wind down," Bingo commented. "But you can still donate to Station 723."

Next up was Q. She entered the Circle of Inquiry. I'd never seen her look more intensely focused.

"One question. One answer. One chance to win it all for the little Aardvarks. Tell me," Bingo asked as he held up the note card with the final question of the tournament on it, "how do you feel, Alice?"

Q gazed out at the audience before responding.

"Perfectly fine."

Then she vomited all over the stage.

Puking is bad. Puking on TV is worse. Fainting and falling into a puddle of your own puke while on TV? Worst of all.

"Holy Sugar Puffs," Bingo exclaimed as he backed away, trying not to get any yakity-yak on his shoes. "Uh, let's take a break." He walked to the upper left-hand corner of the stage. "Call in now to support Station 723," he said into the camera. "Operators are standing by."

The TV crew cut quickly to a prefilmed segment about all the benefits that Station 723 brought to the community. A swarm of us rushed over to Q. I was the first to arrive.

"Q, Q, are you okay?" I raised her head off the floor, careful to avoid the upchuck. "Speak to me."

Slowly, she opened her eyes. They were glassy and red.

"Aardvark."

Phew, I thought, she's going to live, even though there are signs of brain damage.

But she'd had signs of brain damage long before we ever started preparing for the Academic Septathlon, so I wasn't too worried about it.

"Come on, let's get her backstage," Beanpole said.

"No, don't move her!" Miss Terrier ordered, storming over, a cell phone in hand. "An ambulance is on the way."

An ambulance? I thought as the crowd of people around us grew larger. But Miss Terrier wasn't going to take any chances. The last thing she wanted was for the Academic Septathlon to get sued.

Suddenly, Mrs. Applebee fought her way through the crowd.

"Alice? Alice? That's my daughter, let me through." She pushed her way into the ring of people and knelt down to cradle Q in her arms.

"Are you okay? Honey, please tell me you're okay."

"I'm fine, Mom," Q said in a weak voice. "Fine."

"Oh, you are so stubborn," Mrs. Applebee said in a half-scolding, half-relieved voice. "I was sitting out there watching you grow worse and worse, thinking, Why did I even let you do this tonight? Why?"

"Because you love me," Q answered feebly. "But you have to learn to let go, Mom. You're smothering me."

"I'm just so scared to lose you," Mrs. Applebee confessed. Tears ran down her cheeks as she hugged her daughter. "You're all I have left, and I'm just so scared."

"You're not going to lose me, Mom," Q replied. "But you're losing you." Q dragged her arm over her chest and raised the scuba tank to her lips. *Wheeesh-whooosh. Wheeesh-whooosh.* "Like, get a life, Mom. It's kind of pathetic." She smiled weakly.

Mrs. Applebee, the tears still streaming, grinned in response. She knew her daughter was right.

What a nerdwad, I thought. I mean, only Q would have had this kind of conversation with her mother at a time like this.

"Well," Mrs. Applebee said, with uncompromising firmness, "you are done for tonight, miss. Competition's over."

"But—"

"No buts," Q's mom replied. "And no more of those silly homemade homeopathic remedies you've been making for yourself, either. I don't care what it says online about treating nut allergies; we're listening to real doctors from now on."

Beanpole and I turned to one another, looks of shock on our faces.

"But she said that—" Alice protested.

"Excuse me, excuse me, coming through. Give us some space." A paramedic with muscular forearms nudged me out of the way as he knelt down. A moment later, a second EMT, a woman with long, sandy blond hair tied in a ponytail, pulled me up by the shoulder.

"Please, we need some space."

The first paramedic took out a flashlight and started checking Q's vital signs, shining the flashlight at her pupils, taking her blood pressure, that sort of thing. After a short inspection, he took off his stethoscope.

"My guess is they'll probably run an IV to get some fluids in her and then give her something to bring down the fever. She's stable, though. Let's get her on the wagon."

The second paramedic rolled a stretcher onto the stage, put

an oxygen mask over Q's face, and prepared to transport her to the hospital.

"Should I come?" I asked Mrs. Applebee.

"Sorry, only one in the ambulance," the female EMT said to me.

Mrs. Applebee took her cell phone out of her purse. "I'll call you when we get there. You can come later; the hospital's right across the street."

They began to wheel Q off the stage.

"Can't you, like, prop her up or something, for just one more question?" Kiki asked. "It's kind of important."

The paramedic didn't even dignify Kiki's question with a response.

"I'll call you!" I shouted as they rolled Q away.

"Feel better, Alice!" Beanpole yelled. "See you soon."

"And so the twists get more twisty," Bingo said into the camera. "And remember, donation lines are open now. Just take a look at what Station 723 can offer."

Another prerecorded video started to play for the audience as Bingo put down his microphone and a stagehand rushed to clean up the remnants of Q's stomach off the floor.

"Should we go back to our positions now?" Beanpole asked.

"Naw," Bingo replied. "Give it a few more minutes. I mean, look at those phone lines; they're going nuts."

The volunteers who'd been manning the phones were suddenly working at a furious pace. At best, there had been a slow trickle of calls all evening, but now, every single one of the volunteers was on the line, with at least three more phone calls to answer. It was like Station 723 couldn't rake in the cash fast enough.

"People must be calling their friends to say, 'Hey, are you seeing this?'" Bingo explained to us. "Heck, if I'd known this was going to happen, I would have had a kid barf years ago. Take yourselves a little break, ladies. We'll finish up in a few."

Bingo walked off to speak with the stage manager as Wynston and her crew of knee-highs approached, sinister grins painted across their faces.

"Too bad about your little geek pet there," Wynston said in a snide and cutting voice. "Looks like you'll be sending out your big slugger to take her place."

All eyes fell on Sofes. Since we had to remain in the same order, regulations demanded that she be the one to go out there and replace Q for the final question.

"What's that saying, nerdo? Oh, yeah . . . 'Rules are rules.'" Wynston snickered at me, the irony of the whole thing simply too delicious for her. "Come on, Strikers, let's leave them some time to sweat."

The knee-highs mob, smug and tickled by this latest turn of events, sauntered off.

Brattany was the first to speak.

"We're dead. Totally dead."

"No, we're not," Kiki said.

"We're not?" Brattany said. "Are you being sarcastic?"

"Nope, not at all," Kiki replied. "We'll forfeit."

"Forfeit?" I repeated.

"That's right," Kiki told me. "Forfeit." She fluttered her eyelashes and tapped her heart, pretending to be hopelessly distraught. "Due to the emotional strain of having one of our dearest friends and colleagues go to the hospital, we do not think we are fit to go on." She wiped away a fake tear. "And therefore, we'll graciously concede the title to Saint Dianne's." She lowered her head, nobility oozing through the sadness.

A second later, she abandoned the woe-is-me act, stood up tall, and dictated the game plan. "And we do all this knowing, of course, that if the allergy freak hadn't practically poisoned herself, we could have won."

Silence fell over our group as we considered Kiki's strategy.

"I like it," Brattany said, with a devilish smile. "Makes a ton of sense."

"Plus, this way we can avoid the embarrassment of having to send Sofes out there to make a laughingstock of us on live TV," Kiki explained. The fact that Sofes was two feet away from her when she made this comment didn't seem to bother her at all.

"You've got all the angles covered, Keeks," Brattany said, with admiration in her voice. "Double-double nice-nice."

"You mean, I don't have to go answer a question?" Sofes asked timidly, not quite sure about the plan that was being floated.

"Nope," Kiki told her. "You're fine right there." She turned to me. "All right, Captain, go out there and inform the judges."

I paused. Kiki and Brattany were one hundred percent serious. I turned to Beanpole. She wrinkled her brow. "We're gonna forfeit?"

Sofes, embarrassed, ashamed, and kinda confused by the whole thing, twirled her hair and stared at her shoes.

"It's the couldda, wouldda, shouldda excuse," Kiki explained.

"This way, we can always say, 'We couldda, wouldda, shouldda won'... and after seeing the goobwad yak up her small intestine on live TV, who would really argue with us?"

"Hey," Brattany said, growing more and more excited by the moment, "maybe those Moose people will feel sorry for us and give us some money anyway!"

"Do I smell French purses in the air?" Kiki asked with glee. "Maybe we can play on our sad feelings for our friend and at least get half the prize money."

"Like, maybe we could split a purse or something, Keeks!"

"Show me your drowned-puppy-dog look, Brit."

Brattany frowned like her pet turtle had just died.

"Double-double nice-nice," Kiki said, smiling.

I couldn't believe these two.

"You're up, Captain." Kiki nudged me toward the judges. "Go get 'em."

I paused, unable to move.

"Well?" Kiki said. "Go."

Gulp. My feet were frozen to the floor. Each member of the team stared at me. I considered what to do, looking deep into my heart. Suddenly, I realized there was only one way to handle this.

"I gotta pee," I said, and then I raced off to the bathroom before anyone could stop me.

would have thought that a moment alone, to use the restroom, wash my hands, slap some cold water on my face, and sort through my thoughts, would have helped me figure out how the heck to deal with all this.

It didn't.

Sometimes, I guess, the answers in life didn't come; you just had to make a decision and deal with the consequences. I hated those kinds of moments. Made me crave cupcakes.

I decided to do the only thing that made sense: call Mrs. Applebee. I figured taking a moment to check up on Q might help me settle my brain, so I turned on my cell phone and started to dial.

Crud. Inside the bathroom, I had no bars.

I stepped out of the restroom, looking at the screen of my phone, and *boom!* crashed into someone.

My father, to be exact.

"I just need to know one thing," he said, before I'd even had a chance to realize who it was. "Is it okay that I came?"

"What?" I said, disoriented. "How did you get back here?"

Suddenly, Marty appeared.

"Tell him it's not okay, Maureen," my brother insisted. "Tell him it's not okay to abandon his family for his kids' entire lives and then randomly show up one day and think everything gets to be golly-gee-freakin' swell."

"That's not how I am showing up, Marty," my father said.

"That *is* how you are showing up, *Michael*," my brother said. "And we all wish that you'd just disappear. Again. For good."

"Tell you what," my father answered. "If Maureen says she wants me to go, I'll leave right now and never come back." He turned to me. "Say the word, Maureen, and I am gone."

"G'head, Maureen, tell him," Marty said. "Tell him to buzz off."

I . . . I couldn't open my mouth.

"Three minutes until we're back live," the stage manager barked as he cruised past. I looked across at my team standing fifteen feet away. Kiki waved at me to get a move on.

"Just tell him, Maureen," my brother insisted.

"I really can't do this right now," I said. The tension between my dad and my brother was scaring me.

"You have to do this right now," my dad told me. "I'm sorry, Maureen, but you must. I want to be here for you. I know tonight is important, and if I am ever going to be a part of your life, I need to be at things like this." My father put his hand under my chin and raised my face so he could look me in the eye, his voice growing tender and soft. "I know that now, Maureen. It's what I mean by filling holes. But if you tell me to go, well...I will."

"Go!" said Marty.

"Where's Mom and Ashley?" I asked.

"This isn't about them, Maureen," my dad answered. "This is about the fact that you only get one father in this world."

"Or you don't get one," Marty added, nastiness in his tone.

Anger flashed across my father's eyes. Clearly, he'd had just about enough of Marty's commentary.

"The question is, Maureen," he said, "do you want your father to be a part of your life, or do you want your father to leave and never come back?"

"Ninety seconds," called the stage manager.

"Maureen, I'm telling you, if he stays, I am outta here," Marty warned in an ominous voice. What did that even mean, I wondered. Was Marty talking about running away?

Just then, Beanpole walked up. "Sorry to interrupt, Mo, but they need us now." She lowered her voice to a whisper so Kiki couldn't hear her. "Please tell me we're not going to forfeit."

"It's a simple question, Maureen," my father said. "Do you want me to stay, or do you want me to go?"

I gulped.

"I need an answer, dimps. I need an answer right now."

Again with the "dimps." What was with that nickname anyway? I mean, it's not like I had any dimples or anything.

"Thirty seconds," the stage manager called.

"Dimps, the ball is in your court. What's your answer?"

"Like, I know I'm supposed to just accept the universe as it is, but this is unacceptable," Beanpole said.

My father, my brother, Beanpole, the ThreePees, everyone was looking at me, all wanting something. All waiting. Seeing their eyes on me like that, feeling the pressure, well, it made me snap, and suddenly I realized something that I didn't know why I'd never realized before.

There comes a time in a kid's life when people will ask you for stuff that you just can't give them.

"Well, you're not getting an answer now, *Dad*," I said. "You're not getting an answer right now at all." I could feel my blood turning hot. "I mean, you just show up out of nowhere and think that my world has to immediately stop and revolve around you. Well, guess what? It doesn't. That's your answer. Do what you want."

Marty smiled as if he had just won a big victory.

"And you need to stop dragging me into the middle of this," I said, scowling at Marty. "You've got serious issues, dude. How many times did I try to talk to you about this stuff—and *now* you want to talk? So not fair."

I started to walk away, but not without a parting shot. "The two of you, *sheesh*, you must be related."

I left Marty and my father to work it out by themselves. After all, I had other things to deal with.

"So we're forfeiting, right?" Kiki said as I approached, Beanpole following.

"Of course we are," Brattany said, answering the question for me.

A silence came over Beanpole.

Sofes simply twirled her hair and looked down at the floor.

"Shut up, Kiki," I said. "Really, just shut up for once. Sofes," I declared, "you're going out there."

"I am? On TV?"

"She is?" Brattany said.

"Yes, she is," I replied.

"But—" said Kiki.

I thrust my hand at Kiki's face. "I said, shut up. I am the captain, and my decision is that Sophia O'Reilly is going to go out there and represent our school."

Sofes raised her eyes and stared at me. They were big and blue and hopeful and scared. "You think I can do it?" she asked.

"I don't know, Sofes. But I do know that quitting is for cowards." I glared at Kiki. "And Aardvarks may be a lot of things, but we are not cowards. Go out there and do your best."

"Yeah," Beanpole said, perkicized by my attitude. "I mean, do you know how much bravery it takes to stick your nose into an anthill? And think about all those red ants they deal with; that takes even more bravery."

"Um, I think aardvarks eat mostly termites," I said to Beanpole.

"They eat ants, too," she replied confidently. "And locusts and wild cucumber plants and—"

"The point is that they are not quitters," I said, interrupting Beanpole before she relayed to me the entire nutritional regimen of every North American beast with a snout. "Sofes," I commanded, "prepare for victory!"

Just then, Beanpole started to chant.

> *"We're the Aardvarks,*
> *The mighty, mighty Aardvarks!*
> *We're the Aardvarks,*
> *The mighty, mighty Aardvarks!"*

A smile crossed Sofes's face, and I could see her confidence starting to rise.

> *"We're the Aardvarks,*
> *The mighty, mighty Aardvarks!"*

"Positions, please," called the stage manager.

> *"G-o-o-o-o-o, Aardvarks!"*

Beanpole leaped high into the air. "Yay!" she screamed.

"One word," said Kiki, a disgusted look on her face.

"What's that?" asked Brattany, shaking her head in disbelief.

"Laughingstock."

Kiki quietly walked onto the stage and assumed her position at our table. Wynston grinned as Kiki approached, smiling ear to ear. Kiki, her head down, couldn't even muster the strength to acknowledge Wynston's smirk, which was, of course, the biggest acknowledgment of all.

Once again, Wynston Haimes would beat Kiki Masters. This thought, to Wynston, was clearly mouthwatering.

And to Kiki it was clearly unbearable.

The rest of us took our places at the table: Brattany, shoulders slumped; Beanpole, practically jumping out of her skin; Sofes, jittery and nervous; and me, well, I don't know what I was— angry, hyped up, frightened, ready to take on the world, ready to go crawl under my covers and start gulping down microwaved sticky buns. The buzz of all the action had clouded my brainial processing organism.

"Well, it's been a zestfully zesty competition so far, a roller coaster among roller coasters, and now the final finality comes down to this." Bingo paused for dramatic effect as the control-booth guy pushed every button left at his disposal. But he was clearly out of gas. Hardly a swirl of rainbow shimmers remained in the poor fellow.

"Step into the Circle of Inquiry, little Aardvark," Bingo instructed. "This one's for all the marbles."

"She's going to nail it," Beanpole whispered. "I just know it."

"The category is Science," Bingo said, holding up the final blue note card.

"Oh no, not Science," Brattany commented, lowering her head. "That's her worst subject of all."

"Here comes an egg the size of a watermelon," Kiki stated.

"Nice attitude," Beanpole said. "Like, way to support your team."

"I'm just being a realist, Beanpole," Kiki said. "You should try it some time."

"No thanks. Me and Maureen are optimists." She smiled at me. "It's the only way to be at one with the universe, anyway. You can do it, Sofes!" Beanpole cried. "You can do it!"

Was I really an optimist? I mean, if that was true, I was probably the most negative optimist in the history of civilization.

"Grover Park,
Not stupid,
Smart!
Grover Park,
Not stupid,
Smart!
G-o-o-o-o-o, Sophia!"

"Quiet, please," Miss Terrier instructed, speaking into her microphone. "Quiet, everyone."

"And the question is . . .

"Of the 117 known elements in the periodic table of chemical elements, hydrogen is the most abundant in the universe. Oxygen is the third most abundant in the universe. Of the remaining 115, which element in the periodic table is second most abundant?"

Oh, my goodness, I thought, that isn't a question; that's a nuclear bomb.

We'd hardly even covered the periodic table while studying.

All eyes were on Sofes, her face projected on the auditorium screens.

She bit her lip and tried to concentrate.

"Well, hmm, let's see. . . ."

Suddenly, my cell phone buzzed. Of course, it was supposed

to be turned off, but I had turned it on in the bathroom, then jammed it in my pocket and totally forgotten about it. Thank goodness it was set on vibrate.

I ignored the call. Had to. I mean, this was way too intense a moment to answer the phone, and besides, who in the world would...

Oh, no. It was probably Mrs. Applebee, with information about Q. I had to answer.

But I couldn't. Not onstage.

But I had to.

But I couldn't.

"And your response is, Sophia?" Bingo asked.

Sofes, twirling her hair, biting her lip, continued to think. Bingo tried to be patient, but he couldn't wait all day. With each tick of the forty-five-second clock, the pressure grew. My phone buzzed some more.

"Sophia, I need an answer."

"Um," Sofes said, stalling for time, "can I have a definition, please?"

Bingo laughed. "I'm sorry, little Aardvark. They only do that in spelling bees," he said to her with a toothy smile. The audience chuckled, and big grins spread across the faces of Wynston and the girls from Saint Dianne's. Victory was almost theirs. "And your answer is..."

The clock approached eight seconds. My phone stopped vibrating. I'd missed the call.

"Sophia, your time is..."

"Well..." Sofes said, realizing she had to say something or else miss the question entirely. She began to speak, figuring that any kind of answer was better than saying nothing at all. "Since you mentioned the periodic table, you have to have a chair for the table, right? So that's my answer," she reasoned. "The element is the periodic chair."

The periodic chair?

Wynston was the first to blurt out a laugh. Then the rest of the girls from Saint Dianne's giggled, too.

Then Bingo, then the audience. A moment later, laughter filled the entire room.

"I'm sorry, little Aardvark, the answer is helium."

Sofes hung her head.

"And we've got ourselves a CHAMPION! Let's hear it for the Strikers from Saint Dianne's."

The crowd roared. Music began to play, and an explosion of confetti, streamers, and balloons fell from the roof. Sofes, her spirit crushed, moped back to our table as multicolored ribbons, glitter, and sparkles fell on our heads.

The girls from Saint Dianne's jumped high in the air and hugged one another. Their coach ran onstage, joy beaming from her cheeks. I would have thought that coming in second would have been better than coming in third or fourth or even sixth. But it wasn't. Not only had Saint Dianne's just won the Academic Septathlon, Grover Park had just lost it.

Ouch.

My phone buzzed again. Slowly, I reached into my pocket and checked the caller ID. It was Q.

"Hey," I said. "You okay?"

Wheeesh-whooosh. Wheeesh-whooosh.

"Q, is that you? Talk to me?"

I pressed the phone closer to my ear. It was hard to hear through all the commotion.

Wheeesh-whooosh. Wheeesh-whooosh. "There's a new element they recently added to the periodic table."

"What?" I said. "You're not making sense."

"There's a new element called ununseptium. The question's invalid. There are 118 elements in the periodic table, not 117."

"Huh?" I said. "What?" Q must have been following the live-stream feed of the Septathlon over the Internet through her cell phone.

"Protest, Maureen!" she yelled. "You're the captain. Go protest."

I hung up my phone, ran over to the judges' table, pushed my way through the confetti and balloons, and confronted Miss Terrier.

"I protest!" I shouted. "As captain, I protest the question. There are 118 elements in the modern periodic table, not 117. The question's not valid."

Even though I had no idea what in the world I was talking about, Miss Terrier realized she suddenly had a "situation" on her hands, and while the girls from Saint Dianne's were jumping for joy and congratulating themselves under streams of confetti, the judges began having a private conversation.

A moment later, they were checking their computers. Then the regulation guide. Finally, Miss Terrier spoke.

"Grover Park is correct," Miss Terrier said into the microphone, even though it seemed like no one was listening. More than half the audience probably didn't hear, having already risen from their seats to fight the traffic and head home. "The question is invalid."

A ripple of Huh?s and What?s began to filter through the crowd.

"Please return to your seats. Quiet, please. We will be providing another question."

Saint Dianne's suddenly got wind of the fact that something was up. Confused looks crossed their faces.

"What's going on?" asked their coach, approaching the judges.

"The question has been ruled inadmissible, and Grover Park will be provided one more opportunity in the Circle of Inquiry, so, please, everyone, move back to your seats." Miss Terrier tried to reestablish order. "We need quiet in the theater, please."

"What? Why?" Wynston said, coming up to the judges. "What kind of stuff are they trying to pull this time?" she asked, glaring at me.

"It's not 'stuff,'" I said. "The question wasn't valid 'cause there are 118 elements in the periodic table and not 117 like he said."

"Please have your teams return to their positions," Miss Terrier instructed. "Our ruling is final."

Wynston put her hands on her hips and paused. "Fine," she said as she walked past Sofes on her way back to her table. "Ask the girl ten questions. She's not gonna get it right anyway."

Sofes winced.

"They found another stupid technicality, but whatever," Wynston explained to her team. "In forty-five seconds it's not going to matter one bit."

Wynston knocked a yellow balloon out of her way as if this whole thing were just a giant waste of her time.

I had to admit, seeing how frustrated Wynston was made me smile.

Yes! I thought as I walked back to our table. One more chance.

"Nice going, skinny-chubby," Kiki said. "All that achieved was you set us up for another round of embarrassment."

"Yeah," Brattany added, with sad eyes. "Maybe more colored ribbons will fall on our head."

Whoa, I hadn't really thought of it that way. Suddenly, however, I had a brainstorm and rushed back over to the judges' table.

"Can we send out the next member of our team?" I asked. If so, that meant Beanpole would be heading into the Circle of Inquiry. And wait until Saint Dianne's saw that. I pleaded my case. "I mean, we are supposed to keep rotating the order, and it's not our fault that an invalid question was asked, so the rules should allow for—"

"No." Miss Terrier adjusted her glasses. "You may not."

Shot down. I returned to our table. Sofes spoke to me in a low voice. "Does this mean I have to go back out there again?" Her eyes were watery.

I paused before replying; then my shoulders sank. "Not if you don't want to, Sofes. Not if you don't want to."

She swallowed, and I could almost see the lump in her throat.

Sofes turned, first to Kiki, then to Brattany, for guidance. Both of them crossed their arms and stared angrily. Their body language spoke for them.

It was over. It was all over.

Until Beanpole began to chant.

> *"We're the Aardvarks,*
> *The mighty, mighty Aardvarks!*
> *We're the Aardvarks,*
> *The mighty, mighty Aardvarks!"*

Her cheer grew louder.

> *"We're the Aardvarks,*
> *The mighty, mighty Aardvarks!"*

She sang it again louder, now pounding her fists on her thighs.

> *"WE'RE THE AARDVARKS,*
> *THE MIGHTY, MIGHTY AARDVARKS!*
> *WE'RE THE AARDVARKS,*
> *THE MIGHTY, MIGHTY—"*

"I'll do it!" Sofes screamed. "And this time," she said, with fire in her eyes, "I'm gonna victorize us."

I couldn't help shaking my head and cracking a smile. "You do that, Sofes. You go out there and victorize us."

Enthusiastically, she darted off to the Circle of Inquiry.

"Are you serious?" Kiki asked me. "You're letting her go back out there?"

I didn't even acknowledge the question.

"I believe in you, Sophia!" Beanpole called out as Sofes stood at center stage. "I believe in you."

"Me, too, Sofes," I yelled. "Go get 'em! Go show 'em what Aardvarks are made of!"

The girl might not have had the most lightbulbs in her attic, but wow, she had guts.

"The category is still Science." Bingo held up a new blue note card. "And phone lines are still open. By the way, are you familiar with all the benefits that Station 723 brings to the community?"

Another fund-raising promotion appeared on the big screen. The station was milking this for all it was worth.

"Really, you could give that block of wood three-quarters of the answer and she'd still be a quarter short," Wynston said in a voice loud enough for everyone onstage to hear as the promotional video drew to a close.

What a loser, I thought. Smart, pretty, fashionable, and yet what a total loser.

"And now," Bingo said, "the closing conclusion to a remarkable night. The category is Science...."

"When a peroxide-based bleach oxidizes melanin
molecules, it creates an irreversible chemical reaction.
Please identify the effects of this reaction on follicles
of human hair."

"It lightens it, of course," Sofes said, without blinking. "However, if, like, the exposure remains on for too long, lightening turns to burning. That's where we get frosted tips from."

Bingo seemed stunned by the quickness of Sofes's answer. His mouth open, he said nothing.

So Sofes kept talking.

"And then, if you, like, keep the exposure going on certain sections of hair but not on others, you get highlights. But with highlights you've got to be careful to keep the chemicals consistently applied, 'cause otherwise you'd see roots and, like, *yuck* ... like, how tacky are roots?"

Amazed, no one said a word.

"Now, permanent hair coloring, though, is a two-step process. First, you—"

"Um, thank you, Sophia. Your answer is correct. We have a new winner."

Wynston's jaw dropped.

"The victory goes to the little Aardvarks."

Kiki's eyes popped open, and a second later she exploded with a leap into Brattany's arms. The two of them started bouncing and hugging and screaming as Beanpole and I rushed to the Circle of Inquiry to give Sofes a giant hug.

Beanpole, however, tripped over her unevenly sized feet on our way to center stage and ate a faceful of wooden floor.

"Oooh," groaned the audience when they saw how hard she'd fallen.

"Don't worry, don't worry, I'm okay." Beanpole bounced up and turned to me. "Did it leave a mark?"

"Nahhh," I said, even though there was a cruise ship on her forehead.

"You did it, Sofes. You did it!" Beanpole hugged Sofes like she'd never hugged a friend before. Joy radiated from their faces as if they'd just won a three-hundred-million-dollar lottery.

I rushed to join in the celebration, jumping and screaming and hugging.

"GROVER PARK,
NOT STUPID,
SMART!
GROVER PARK,
NOT STUPID,
SMART!"

"Eat that, Wynston!" Kiki barked. "I mean, how you like me now, girlfriend?" she added, wagging her head at Wynston, really rubbing it in.

"And put some spank on it!" Brattany added as the two of them high-fived.

"Double-double nice-nice!"

Just then I realized that for Kiki, the best part of all of this didn't come from winning; it came from Wynston's losing.

Pah-thetic.

"Make sure you show your little boo-hoo to the audience, Winnie," Kiki said as she pointed at one of the television cameras, "'cause donation lines are still open."

Kiki and Brattany stuck out their tongues and ran to join us in the Circle of Inquiry.

Of course, no streamers fell from the rafters. We got no confetti or balloons or even music. They'd used all that stuff up already. The whole Civic Center was eerily quiet. But did the little Aardvarks care?

Not at all.

"Great job, Sofes!" Kiki exclaimed, ready to smother her in a hug.

"You were awesome," said Brattany.

Sofes stiffened.

"Get away from me," she said in a disgusted voice. A cold, heartless glare fell like a shadow across her face. "And don't touch me, Keeks." She held up her hand.

Kiki stepped backward, confused. "Huh?"

"Just stay away from me, the two of you," Sofes told them. "I'm a—" She paused, then looked at Beanpole and me. "I think I'm a Nerd Girl."

One at a time, Sofes pulled the two fancy green barrettes out of her hair and threw them down on the stage floor.

"Matter of fact," she said. "I'm positive."

Sofes turned back to Beanpole and me. "I think I owe you guys an apology."

tanding onstage, I had only one thought floating through my mind.

"Wow, we won. We really won."

But as we found out the next day, actually, we hadn't. Back at school, drama was in the air.

All over school.

To start with, Wynston had protested everything. After reviewing the videotape of the contest, she officially objected to our protest, since we'd only disputed the question about the periodic table because of the fact that I had illegally answered a phone call while onstage, which, of course, was cause for our team's immediate disqualification.

"But the contest was over," I pleaded.

"Not if you were going to protest, it wasn't," Miss Terrier informed me as we all sat in Mr. Mazer's office. "I guess I didn't see you do that, because of all the balloons." Miss Terrier had made a special trip to our school in order to explain everything to us. Apparently, there were a lot of pieces to this puzzle.

"Additionally, the tape confirmed that one of the judges nodded permission for Wynston to exchange calculators, so when she originally violated the rules, she did so with a judge's approval." On her laptop computer monitor, Miss Terrier showed us a slow-motion replay of what had happened.

Yep, sure enough, the potbellied judge had nodded his head when Wynston raised her calculator after her batteries had died, as if he were giving her permission to swap devices. The videotape made that crystal clear.

"So, really," Miss Terrier said, "the point deduction wasn't ever warranted."

"But that's not fair," Kiki complained. "I mean, we won, and now you're telling us we didn't. That prize money belongs to us."

I rolled my eyes. Kiki had probably already ordered her stupid purse, even though we hadn't been given any cash yet. As with all stuff like this, they never gave you the money that night; the check was always "in the mail."

"Yeah," Brattany added. "And my dad's a lawyer."

Hearing Brattany say that for the forty-thousandth time caused Q to groan. All in all, Q had spent less than four hours in the hospital. Once they got her hydrated and gave her an injection of some antihistamines in order to counteract the nuts she'd overexposed herself to, she'd returned to good old-fashioned *Wheeesh-whooosh. Wheeesh-whooosh* form. Didn't even miss a day of school.

Miss Terrier reached into her purse, having already worked out a solution.

"Due to the confusion, we've decided to split the prize money this year. Saint Dianne's will get half and Grover Park will get the other half. Congratulations, Aardvarks," Miss Terrier said. "You surprised a lot of people."

She passed me the envelope. Smiling, I tore it open.

"Wow, one thousand seven hundred and fifty dollars." I'd never held so much money in my entire life.

Kiki and Brattany grinned from ear to ear. Half was better than nothing, right?

"And as captain," I said, attempting a formal announcement, "it's my pleasure to inform you that the Grover Park Aardvarks Academic Septathlon team would like to donate this check to the art department."

"What?!" Fire flashed across Kiki's eyes.

"We know budgets are tight," I said to Mr. Mazer. "And we know that our reckless, thoughtless, immature behavior caused the school some extra expenses it really couldn't afford." I handed Mr. Mazer the check. "We hope you'll accept our apology."

I put my arm around Kiki's shoulder, hugging her tight. "We Aardvarks were wrong."

Kiki threw my arm off her shoulder, not even bothering to fake a grin.

"Well, well, well," Mr. Mazer said as he held the prize money in his hand. "It does seem as though a lesson or two was learned in all this, does it not, Mr. Piddles?"

"Indeed it does," Mr. Piddles replied, with an approving nod of his head. "Matter of fact, I'd go so far as to say that justice has prevailed." He glanced over at the vacant chair in the corner of the room where Vice Principal Stone usually sat.

Today the chair was empty. "Justice, I believe, has been served across the board."

Though he was only months from retirement, Mr. Stone, we'd learned earlier that morning, had been placed on administrative leave because of his unprofessional conduct toward our team.

"Of course I ratted him out to Mr. Piddles," I'd told Kiki earlier that day, when she'd confronted me about it after first period. News about scandals at school traveled with such lightning speed that the gossip about Mr. Stone had already entered the ears of every kid on campus by the start of second period. "Why wouldn't I?" I continued. "There's a difference between snitching and standing up for yourself when someone's being an abusive, bullying jerkwad. Screw Mr. Stone."

"But he's gonna zap us," Kiki answered.

"Show some spine," I responded. "Guy's a putz."

"You had no right," Brattany said.

"What are you complaining about?" Q told her. "Your dad's a *law-yerrr*."

"True dat," Brattany replied. "But he's not gonna defend you."

"Come on, guys. Can't we just get along?"

Sofes nodded in agreement. "Yeah, get along like those kayakers who had to drink the protein shakes."

Huh? We all stared.

"Well, maybe it was soy," Sofes clarified, as if that made better sense.

Things, as anyone could tell, had gone right back to being

just as they'd always been between the ThreePees and the Nerd Girls, which was why handing the check over to Mr. Mazer felt just so delicious to me.

"We're proud to make the donation, sir," I said. "It feels... how do you say?" I asked Q.

"Double-double nice-nice."

"Yeah," I repeated. "Double-double nice-nice."

Steam was practically coming out of Kiki's ears as she watched Mr. Mazer place the check inside his desk drawer.

"Of course, we can only send one team from our region to represent us in the state competition," Miss Terrier informed us.

"Just one?" I said, hoping we'd get the chance to go on to the finals. I know, I know—what a nerd, right? I mean, who else but a total dorkasaurus actually wants more study pain on their plate? But it was fun.

"You should send Saint Dianne's."

I whirled around to see who'd said that.

"Saint Dianne's should go," Sofes continued. "They're better than us and they deserve it."

Instead of wearing a shimmering, shiny outfit today, Sofes was dressed in a simple white T-shirt with jeans. Her hair, of course, looked styled and nice in a tight, clean ponytail, and she wore a few cool bracelets, but she wasn't poufed out to the max like she usually was.

Beanpole nodded her agreement. "It's true. They earned it."

Sofes smiled at Beanpole, Beanpole smiled at Sofes, and the two of them shook their heads in unison, their ponytails—the same length, the same color rubber band—bobbing up and down at the same time. It was like the two of them were long-lost sisters born to a mother whose brain hadn't gotten enough oxygen at the time of their birth.

"Maybe we'll join a new squad of some sort," Sofes suggested.

"Yeah, like, something academic and rigorous," Beanpole replied.

"I know, a cookie-baking club!" Sofes exclaimed.

That's her idea of rigorous and academic? I thought.

"Oh, wait until you see the architectural wonders my mom can do with lemon bars," Beanpole informed her.

Kiki and Brattany rolled their eyes. The ThreePees were officially down to two.

"Well, that settles it," Miss Terrier said. "I'll inform the team from Saint Dianne's that they will be our regional representatives."

"Tell them they're the real winners," I said. "I think it's important they know that we said that about them."

Kiki fumed.

"Shall do," Miss Terrier confirmed as she picked up her purse, preparing to leave. "And perhaps we'll see you for the high school competition next year, ladies?"

"You might," I said.

"Or not," Kiki snipped.

After saying good-bye to Miss Terrier, the six of us departed the principal's office and got ready to go to lunch. But before the ThreePees and the Nerd Girls parted ways, Kiki had to launch one final missile.

"This is not over, skinny-chubby," she said. "There's still a lot of time left in eighth grade. Be warned."

"Stuff it in your purse, Kiki," I replied. "Your non-French one, that is."

Q snorted.

Brattany glowered. "My dad's a lawyer."

"So's my mom," Q said.

"She is not," Brattany said.

"Is too," Q replied. "She just stopped practicing a few years ago." She turned to me. "But we talked, and, well, she's going to start working again. Part-time."

I smiled.

"My dad will still sue her," Brattany said in a superior sort of way.

"Your dad should sue himself for raising such a booger for a kid," Q answered. Brattany's jaw practically fell to the floor. "And he can sue her mom, too," Q added, pointing at Kiki. "It'll be a class-action lawsuit, a guaranteed win."

"Come on, guys," Beanpole said. "Can't we all just get along?"

Kiki's response was short, crisp, and to the point.

"*Pfft.*"

I watched as the *two* ThreePees wiggled off to their usual lunch table. Sofes, however, stayed with us as we cruised over to our spot in the back corner of the courtyard. For the first time ever, all the seats at our table were filled.

Kiki and Brattany ate alone, quietly. It was weird not seeing a flurry of action around them. Almost as weird as it was to have our table feel like a hotbed of activity.

Beanpole and Sofes talked a mile a minute, comparing phones, chatting about how they liked to organize their sock drawer. The two of them had a million things in common. Q, of course, was back on the deflavorized food wagon.

"Tofu cubes?" I asked when she removed a Tupperware container from her lunch sack.

"The battle may be lost, but the war is not over." Q jabbed her spork into a slice of skinless pear. "Today fruit, tomorrow..." she said, looking at my lunch, "pizza." She smiled and put the sporked piece of pear in her mouth. "The low-fat kind, of course."

"It's Giuseppe's," I answered, defending my nutritional choice. "My dad brought it over last night."

"More hole-filling, huh?" Beanpole asked.

"Well, I'm certainly filling my hole right now," I said as I took a big, cheesy bite of pizza. "And I don't care if I don't have another glass of water for an entire month."

Beanpole shot me one of her famous motherly looks. I knew she wanted me to spill more details, but couldn't she see I was eating?

"There's something about a great bite of pizza that makes every last calorie worth it," I said as the flavorful pizza grease drizzled over my tongue.

Beanpole continued to stare.

"What?" I said, chewing.

"Do I need to mention the name of a certain condiment again?" she asked.

Sofes wrinkled her brow, evidently having no idea what we were talking about.

I heaved a sigh and set down my lunch. "Okay, okay, I know he's trying to make up for years of lost time by going for my weak spot," I said. "But I did tell him last night that nothing was going to just magically happen. If he and I were going to be cool with one another, we were going to have to go slow."

I wiped my hands with a napkin.

"You said that?" Beanpole asked.

"I did."

"Just like that?" she asked.

I nodded.

"How very unketchuplike," she replied, with a smile. She stood up and began to walk over to me. "I'm proud of you, Mo."

"Don't hug me. Don't hug me.... Oh, you hugged me. *Awk*ward."

"What can I say? I'm a hugger," Beanpole replied with a grin.

"I'm a hugger, too," Sofes said. The two of them looked at each other, and then—what else?—decided to hug.

Unfortunately, they each turned the same way, leaned eagerly forward, and *BAM!* smashed their foreheads in a head-on collision.

"Ouch!" they yelped at the same time.

"Don't worry, don't worry, I'm okay," said Beanpole.

"Um, me too, I think," Sofes said, rubbing her melon. Both of them looked at me.

"Did it leave a mark?"

"Barely noticeable," I replied, looking at the red tree stump each of them was growing. "Hardly detectable at all."

"So, you're going to give him a chance?" Q asked, in reference to my father.

"Uh-huh. But I also told him that if he was going to try to use me to get to Marty, well . . . that wasn't happening." I reached for a sip of my Mountain Dew. Ounce for ounce, I think, Mountain Dew has more sugary fizz than any other soda on the market. Plus, it's green, and green foods, as every doctor says, are good for you.

Beanpole stared, waiting for more. I could tell by the look on her face that she didn't believe me.

"It's true," I said. "Beyond that, we didn't really talk much. Marty came back, and the two of them are a disaster. But my dad did ask if I want to go to a basketball game with him this season; said he could get good tickets to the NBA. We're a work in progress, I guess."

I gulped down a second swig of soda and then took another chomp of Giuseppe's famous extra-cheesy pizza.

"Hi, Maureen," said Logan, walking up to our table

"*Glrrmmff mlimpfft*," I answered, caught between bites, trying to swallow.

"Can I, like, talk to you for a sec?" he asked, edging toward a tree that was about twenty feet away. Sofes, Beanpole, and Q giggled.

"Um, sure," I said, quickly wiping my chin. We walked away to chat in private.

"I got you something," he said, handing me a box.

"You did?"

He got me a gift? I took the small, square package but hesitated before opening it.

"Please tell me it's not a wedding ring," I said. "'Cause I really think we should live together first."

"Naww," Logan replied with a smile. "It's not a wedding ring. Weddings are stupid."

Well, I wouldn't have gone that far. I opened the box.

"Whoa, a State Championship Academic Septathlon medal," I said, holding up the blue ribbon on which a tarnished silver medallion hung. I looked more closely. It was discolored, and the piece certainly had lost its shine, but emblazoned across the front, the medal clearly read CAPTAIN.

"Where'd you get it?"

"Turns out my dad was captain of his Septathlon team about a hundred years ago, and when he saw the contest on channel 723, and he saw you, well...he wanted me to give it to you," Logan told me. "Said, when I got home that night...Naw, I'm embarrassed to say."

"What?" I said. "Tell me."

"He said I'd picked a winner to have a crush on."

My heart melted.

"And he didn't mean it like pick a booger, either."

"Yeah, uh, I kinda got that, Logan."

"Do you think maybe I can walk you home from school today?" he asked. "I mean, not like, carry your books or anything, 'cause that would be stupid. Heck, books are stupid. Not like video games. Video games are not stupid, but—"

"Yes," I said, interrupting him. "I'd love for you to walk me home from school today." I stared at the championship medallion.

"Cool." Logan's blue eyes sparkled. "I'll meet you at the front gate."

"See you, then," I said. Logan trotted back to his group of friends, and I floated back to my lunch table, my head in the clouds.

"Oooh, there's gonna be some smoochy-smoochy," Q teased.

A smile felt as if it had been permanently stamped on my face.

"What'd he give you? What'd he give you?" Beanpole asked, taking the box from me. "Wow. Captain." She looked up. "You deserve it, Mo."

"Yeah," said Sofes. "Like, you taught me to be an optometrist."

"You mean an optimist."

"Exactly, Captain," Sofes replied. "You taught me to be an optimist."

Q reached over, took the medallion from Beanpole, and inspected its details. A moment later, she passed it back to me and nodded approvingly. "Aardvark."

I grinned and picked up my slice of pizza. *Mmm*, how much did I love Giuseppe's?

I walked to the garbage and threw my entire lunch away, soda and all.

"What's the matter?" Beanpole asked.

"I know what the matter is," Q said.

Everyone turned.

"Maureen's in"—*Wheeesh-whooosh. Wheeesh-whooosh*—"love."

I flushed. It was time to stop kidding myself, I thought. Eat good, feel good. I mean, how long had I been violating one of life's simplest rules?

"Tell us, tell us, when are you going to see him again?" Beanpole asked.

"After school. He's walking me home."

"Awww," said Beanpole, leaning backward. "So romantic." But she leaned too far backward and fell off the bench.

Thud.

"Don't worry, don't worry, I'm okay," she said, scrambling back up. "I may still need a few more tai chi classes."

"Or a wardrobe made of protective body armor," I offered.

"Can I just say something?" Sofes asked as she reached over and pulled a leaf out of Beanpole's hair.

"Of course you can," Beanpole replied, a twig still dangling from her curls.

"Nerds are fun."

"We're not just fun," I replied. "Nerds rule."